Even A Little Is Something

Even A Little Is Something

Stories of Nong

by Tom Glass

Illustrated by Elena Gerard

Linnet Books
1997

First published 1997 as a Linnet Book,

an imprint of The Shoe String Press, Inc.,

North Haven, Connecticut 06473.

Library of Congress Cataloging-in-Publication Data

Glass, Tom, 1958–

Even a little is something : stories of Nong / Tom Glass ;

illustrated by Elena Gerard.

p. cm.

Summary: Twenty-three vignettes present Nong, an eleven-year-old girl

living in present-day Thailand, and the characters of her village as

they slowly make the transition from rural poverty to western

modernization.

ISBN 0-208-02457-3 (lib. bdg. : alk. paper)

[1. Thailand—Fiction.]   I. Gerard, Elena, ill.   II. Title.

PZ7.G48126Et   1997

[Fic]—DC21   97-21878

CIP

AC

The paper in this publication meets the minimum requirements

of American National Standard for Information Sciences—

Permanence of Paper for Printed Library Materials,

ANSI Z39.48—1984. ⊗

Designed by Abigail Johnston

Printed in the United States of America

For My Family

Contents

❀ Part One

The *Somtam*

NONG LIVED with her mother and sister in a wooden house down the lane. Like most of the families in their village, they had a dirt floor. When Nong came home on her bicycle, she could turn in from the lane and ride straight into her house. She liked doing that so much that she often went back out and came home again.

In front of their house was a papaya tree that sometimes bore fruit. Out back were other fruit trees and a well. Also out back was their kitchen. When Nong's mother cooked, the smell of the food drifted out through the neighborhood. In their village, all of the kitchens were in back of the houses. Families who were cooking special meals always made extra, in case someone else smelled the good food and stopped in.

Nong's house, with its dirt floor and its kitchen, was in a province called Mahasarakham, in northeastern Thailand. All over the province were houses in villages like Nong's, surrounded by ricefields turning dusty under the sun.

On Saturdays Nong's mother sent her to the corner to buy papaya salad, or *somtam*, from a woman called Aunt Ray. The lane was dusty, and Nong had to ride along squinting. She was eleven years old.

One Saturday her mother said, "I don't have any money right now. Tell Aunt Ray that we'll pay for the *somtam* tomorrow."

Nong rode to the corner and ordered the *somtam*. Aunt Ray pounded the chili peppers and garlic with a mortar and pestle. She added fish sauce and shredded papaya, and she pounded that, too. When Aunt Ray scooped it out of the mortar and into a plastic bag, Nong reached into her pocket.

"Where's my money?" she said. "My mother gave me a coin, but now I can't find it." She looked around in the dust and under Aunt Ray's wooden stand.

"It's all right, Nong," said Aunt Ray. "You can pay me the next time."

Back at home, Nong poured the *somtam* onto a plate. She and her mother sat down to eat it on a mat that was spread on the dirt floor, not very far from her bicycle.

Nong's older sister, Oi, sat down and joined them. Oi was already seventeen.

"Something is wrong with this *somtam*," said Oi. "What's different about it?"

"We didn't pay for it," said her mother. "That's what is different."

"We got it for free?"

Nong shook her head. "We got it by sinning." She told them about the lie she had told to Aunt Ray.

"You didn't need to lie," said her mother. "Not having money is nothing to be ashamed of."

"It isn't even really a sin," said Oi. "This *somtam* isn't enough to fill us. It's only a sin if you lie to get more than you need." She took another bite of the *somtam*—a small bite, so that she wouldn't look greedy.

"Is that true?" asked Nong, who wanted to learn more about sinning.

At that moment Oi let out a cry and put her hand up to her mouth. "A stone," she said as her eyes watered. She turned her head away and spit out a small black pebble into her hand. "It chipped my tooth."

"It's nothing," said their mother. "Look how small it is." To back up her words she helped herself to more *somtam*, although she studied it carefully before putting it into her mouth.

"My tooth hurts," said Oi. She ran her tongue over the new roughness.

"It's because of my sin," thought Nong.

That afternoon Oi rode the bicycle downtown. Nong sat behind her, on the metal rack over the back tire. It was really Nong's bicycle, and Oi's knees stuck out as she pedaled.

The dentist was in his waiting room saying goodbye to a patient when they rode up. A receptionist sat at a counter.

"What a day," said the dentist as they went in. He went out on the sidewalk, lit up a cigarette, and smoked.

"It will be just a minute," said the receptionist.

Nong and Oi sat on a bench in the waiting room. They thought about their mother, left alone in their house. They often thought about her as they sat in their classrooms at school. They wondered what she was doing at the time and how she was feeling. It seemed like a natural thing for daughters to do.

The dentist finished smoking and led them to the back room. Nong watched as Oi sat in the chair and opened her mouth. The dentist smoothed out the roughness with a tool. Then they went out to the counter.

The receptionist told them the fee, and they nodded. Oi reached into her pocket.

"Where is the money?" Oi turned to Nong. "Did I give it to you?"

"No," said Nong confidently, for she was not lying.

They looked around on the floor and behind the counter. "Can we pay you tomorrow?" asked Oi. "We lost our money."

The receptionist took them back to the dentist again. "He's been kind to too many people already," she said, and they went in.

The dentist was looking into a new patient's mouth. "These girls say they can't find their money," the receptionist told him.

The dentist picked up a tool from a tray without looking down from the mouth.

"How much did you lose?" he asked.

Both Nong and Oi stood there. Neither of them could think of a number.

The dentist was still looking into the new patient's mouth. "What if I bought your bicycle?" he said. "And then I couldn't find my money? Would you still let me take it? Of course you wouldn't. That would be stealing. You would make me pay first."

"It's an old bicycle," said Nong. "You wouldn't want to buy it."

For the first time, the dentist looked down at them. "I'm not going to unfix your tooth. But if you find your money, please pay me. All right? I can be kind, but I'm not always happy." And he bent back down to his patient.

Nong and Oi got on their bicycle in front of the office.

"Well, we sinned again," said Nong as they rode away. "Now we can never go back to see him."

Oi was pedaling with her knees sticking out. "We can find some money. We'll pay."

"No, we won't. If we get any money, we'll spend it on blankets. Winter is coming up soon."

"What if you get a toothache? What will you do then? Will you be too proud to go to the dentist?"

Nong sat behind Oi with her arms folded. "I won't get a toothache, that's all."

"You'd better watch what you chew then," said Oi as she ran her tongue over her tooth.

Mr. Pu

WHEN NONG WENT DOWN the dirt lane one way, she came to Aunt Ray's *somtam* stand. But if she went the other way, toward the canal, she passed the house of the old man everyone called Mr. Pu.

Most of the houses on that lane were made of wood, with dirt floors. Nong's house was like that. But the floor of Mr. Pu's house was made of cement. Still, dust blew in. A woman who stayed there swept it out. Nong did not know that woman's nickname.

If no one was looking, Nong went into the house to see Mr. Pu.

He wore a checked cloth tied around his waist. He sat on the floor, and the woman who swept brought him tea.

"How aren't you today?" he greeted Nong. "Are you married or not yet?"

Nong sat across the room from him, in the shadows. His white hair was cut short, and she could see his ribs easily.

"Remember when my parents were your age?" asked Mr. Pu. "My father was a mango tree then. My mother was the wheel of an oxcart. No, no, that was my pet pineapple."

After he drank some tea, he looked across at Nong. "Tell me," he said.

Nong stared at him, and Mr. Pu nodded. "Just as I thought." He

smiled at Nong, showing his brilliant white teeth. Then he tilted his head toward the back of the house. "Bring in some stew soup!" he called out.

Nong knew that there was something about Mr. Pu. Her mother told her not to go see him. "Go out and exercise," she said. "Don't go that way down the lane."

Nong had seen Mr. Pu leave his house only once. He had taught her a song that day: "My jello is yellow; my umbrella is blue," is how the song went. Nong sang along with him, moving her lips without really saying the words. When she got up to go, Mr. Pu stood, too.

"Now where is my jello?" he was saying. That was when he went outside. He looked in a papaya tree. "Not up there." He peeled a banana and looked in the skin. "Not in there." He looked around in the dust beside the dirt lane.

Then he looked at Nong. "Do you have it? Do you have my jello is yellow?" He took a step toward her. "I knew it was you," he exclaimed.

Nong gave a cry and ran up the lane toward her house. When she looked back, Mr. Pu was standing right where he had been, in front of his house. He was smiling again, showing his teeth. He was waving goodbye.

"From now on, I'll call you Jello," Mr. Pu shouted.

Maybe one reason Nong liked Mr. Pu was that she did not have a father. Her own father had died. He used to sit on their floor at home, wearing a checked cloth around his waist, too. His skin had been less sagging and wrinkled than Mr. Pu's. It had come as a surprise to everyone when Nong's father died.

After that, Nong's mother spent more and more time by herself. But Nong learned to go down to see Mr. Pu.

Mr. Pu was sitting there waiting for her. "Ah, Jello. Come out."

She sat down. She noticed the dust more on the cement floor in his house than she did on the dirt floor at home.

Mr. Pu took a long sip from a glass. He gave a satisfied nod. "It's coconut cola," he said. "You know, every time I drink coconut cola, someone I like will come see me. And now look. Here you are!" He held up the glass and took another long sip. He seemed to be winking at her. Or maybe that was the reflection of the drink in his eyes.

Mr. Pu leaned toward her. "You're sitting in the shadows. I can't see you."

Nong sat still on the floor.

"Oh! You're angry because I didn't give you a glass of coconut cola. Well, I can do better than that." He tilted his head and called out, "Bring in the icicle cream!"

The woman who swept brought in a bowl. Then she went out. Mr. Pu put the bowl down on the floor.

"It's for you," he said.

Nong sat looking at the bowl.

"It's bad luck to let icicle cream melt," Mr. Pu went on. "One of my wives let some melt once, and from that day on she kept growing older. Or was that my black cat? Well, they had the same number of wings."

"I'd like some," said Nong.

"Good question!"

"But my mother doesn't let me eat dessert before supper."

"Then don't 'eat' it, Jello. 'Nibble' it. 'Partake of' it. 'Feast on' the icicle cream! Do anything but 'eat' it, Jello. Make sure you don't disobey your mother."

Nong slid toward the bowl.

But Mr. Pu pulled it back. "First, you have to say the magical word."

"Please?"

Mr. Pu shook his head. "The magical word," he said, "is 'I promise to wash the bowl when I finish the icicle cream!'" He held the bowl out toward her. "Can you say that magical word?"

"Sure," said Nong, and she reached out.

But Mr. Pu was holding onto the bowl. He shook it a little. The icicle cream shivered, like jello. "It's melting," he said. "You have to say the magical word yourself."

Nong felt herself smiling. "I promise to wash the bowl when I finish the icicle cream!" Her voice sounded louder than she had expected it to.

Mr. Pu nodded slowly. "Ah. Now that is the magical word." He put the bowl down. "Let the feast begin!"

Nong took the bowl. Mr. Pu watched as she ate—as she partook of—the icicle cream.

That Day

NONG AND HER FRIENDS often talked about the day when they had gone around riding their bicycles. "Remember That Day?" they would say.

Nobody could remember how That Day had begun, or how they had gotten together. All they could remember was that suddenly there they all were, riding down their dirt lane, pedaling faster and faster.

One of the boys looked back. "Look at the dust!" he shouted.

It was true. Together, riding fast, they were raising a trail of dust, just like a motorcycle. A bicycle doesn't raise dust going slowly. A bicycle doesn't raise dust alone.

They rode on, glancing back.

"Faster!" shouted someone, and that raised more dust.

They turned and rode alongside the canal, all the way to the next village. There was dust all the way. Then a woman in one of the cement houses across the canal shouted out.

"Hey, you kids!" she said. "Come on over here for some mango cookies!"

The cookies were still warm from the oven. "You're in such a hurry," said the woman. "Where are you off to?" She brought out plate after plate of the cookies. Nong and her friends chewed even harder than they had pedaled. Then they were back on their bikes.

They went on down the lane, powered by the fresh mango cookies. They finally stopped at a rickety footbridge. None of them had ever ridden that far before.

"We're not afraid," they agreed, and they went out on the footbridge.

Nong had picked a blade of grass from the bank; she threw it down to the canal. A fish came up for it.

"Maybe he thought it was a mango cookie," said one of the boys.

Then they were back on their bicycles. They turned down a side lane and stood up as they rode, for more power. Sometimes they pedaled so hard that their bicycles lurched to the side and almost fell over.

This lane cut through ricefields. The fields were dry, and the soil had been baked white. Sometimes in the shade Nong saw water in the bottom of a pond as she turned to glance back at their dust.

Down by one of the drying-up ponds sat a boy and a girl.

"Hey!" They stopped their bikes and called down. "Want to join us?"

The boy and girl shook their heads. "We're brother and sister," they said. "We're watching our buffalo."

"OK!" Nong and her friends watched the buffalo stand up and stretch all its legs. The buffalo was green from the scum of the water.

Then they were riding away. This time they pedaled even harder, so that the boy and the girl with the buffalo would see the dust and regret not having come with them.

They turned down another side lane that angled back to the canal. They went back the way they had come, raising the same dust, passing the footbridge, waving at the woman who baked mango cookies. They came up to their own lane and rode right on past.

They rode alongside the canal until, without saying anything, they all turned and rode through the gate of the temple.

Their village did not have much money, but there was always enough to keep up the temple. The white walls and the orangish-red roof shone out against the dust of their village.

A monk came over to them. Though they were panting, they tried to breathe softly.

"Hey, you kids," said the monk. "Want something to drink?"

He led them to a clay jar in the shade of a mango tree.

"This is genuine water," he said. "It will go down your throats smoothly."

They took turns dipping in a cup and drinking the real water.

"Don't gulp," the monk told them. "The water isn't going any-where."

He looked over at their bicycles. "I haven't ridden a bicycle in ages. Where did you ride to today?"

"Just around," they said.

The monk nodded. "Well, one place is as good as the next."

Whenever Nong and her friends talked about That Day, they said the same things. Somebody talked about the footbridge. Somebody mentioned the fish, somebody the green buffalo, somebody the cookies. Then they fell silent, and that is when everyone was thinking of the monk at the temple.

"If you have to rest this long," he told them as they sat in the shade, "you must have been riding too hard. Learn to work some rest into whatever you're doing. You won't get so tired that way." He wandered off. He seemed to be resting even as he walked.

Nong and her friends tried resting as they pedaled back home.

"It's working," said someone. "I'm not getting tired at all."

"Yeah," said one of the boys, "but we're not raising any dust, either."

None of them could argue with that. In fact, nobody said anything the rest of the way home. And, as it turned out, they never rode around the way they had on That Day again.

Ironing

NOW THAT NONG WAS IN FIFTH GRADE, she had to wash clothes. That was her new household chore. She put her own clothes along with her mother's and her sister's in a metal tub in back of their house and scrubbed them clean on a washboard. She hung them over the railing in front of their house in the morning, then moved them around back later on, to catch the afternoon sun. While the clothes were drying, Nong stayed on the lookout for rain.

Her older sister, Oi, got a job at one of the new cement houses across the canal. The rice paddies over there were being filled in and built up as suburbs.

Oi's job was ironing clothes. She sat cross-legged on the floor and used a low ironing board, only a foot or so high. She worked two days a week after school, and Nong went with her.

"Don't sit there," the woman in the house said to Nong. "That sofa is new, can't you see?" The woman's name was Khun Supaporn.

Nong sat on the tiled floor next to Oi as Khun Supaporn went out of the room. "I could work, too," said Nong. "I could wash the clothes and give them to you."

"They have a washing machine," said Oi.

Nong watched her iron. "Those are big pants."

17

"They're Khun Supaporn's husband's."

"So he is fat?"

"It's none of our business what he looks like."

"Well, it means more work for you."

Oi finished the pants, then took a pair of underwear from the basket.

"Now what are you going to do?" Nong asked.

"I have to iron his underwear. That's what Khun Supaporn told me."

Nong watched Oi spread out the large pair of briefs. And the next day, as Nong washed her own clothes, she thought about that. She had never known people who ironed their underwear. On the other hand, she had never asked anyone. Maybe it was a commonplace thing.

She wondered if her teachers ironed their underwear. She doubted that her friends did. But she had never asked them. It was too silly a subject to bring up.

One night as Oi ironed their own family's clothes, on the wooden floor upstairs, Nong brought a pair of her underwear in and laid it in front of Oi. "Please iron my underwear," she said.

Oi was ironing the blouse of her school uniform. "No."

"But you iron Khun Supaporn's husband's."

"That's my job. I have to do that."

Nong smoothed out the underwear on the ironing board. "Look how small they are. It wouldn't even take thirty seconds."

Oi was busy with the pleats of the sleeves of the blouse. "I spend too much time ironing already." Gnats flew in and landed on the blouse. Oi had to flick them off, so that they wouldn't be ironed into the fabric.

"I'm your sister," said Nong.

Oi gripped the iron harder. She was ironing the same spot over

and over, where her name was stitched into the blouse. "I don't even like ironing," she said. "But I can't do anything else. What other job can I get?" She dug the point of her iron into the stitching and dragged it across her full name. "Ironing is becoming my life."

A tear fell onto the blouse. Oi ironed it away.

Nong sat watching her. "It's all right," she said. "You don't have to iron my underwear." She picked them up.

Oi rubbed her eyes. "No, I'll do them. I'm better now." She held out her hand. "Give them to me."

Nong turned away. "No. I can see now. It's silly. Who ever heard of ironing underwear?"

"It's nothing," said Oi. "I don't mind. Give them here."

Nong shook her head. "Why don't you finish your blouse?"

"Ironing underwear." Oi was looking off, out the window. "I get paid for ironing underwear." She shook her head. "That's how I make my living." She gave the signs of a smile. "That's my career."

"There are lots of worse things you could do."

"Oh, sure. I can hold my head up proudly. People will say, 'There goes that girl Oi. She's the underwear ironer, isn't she?' We could put a sign up in front of the house." She drew the outline of a sign in the air. " 'Madame Oi. Underwear Ironed—And Folded'!"

" 'Best Rates In Town'!"

" 'Emergency Service Available'!"

By now they were laughing. Nong was still holding her pair of unironed underwear.

"You could charge by the kilo," she said.

"I could charge by the waist size!"

Nong began laughing harder. She was picturing a big scale downstairs, piled high with oversized underwear. She fell back on the floor, laughing. "Ironing underwear!" she said. Oi fell back, too, after she

20

made sure that the iron was sitting upright—for she was, after all, a professional.

Soon their mother came up from downstairs, where she had been gossiping with neighbors. "What happened?" she asked.

Oi tried to sit up. "Nong won't let me iron her underwear." She and Nong burst out laughing again.

Their mother raised her eyebrows. Then she went back down the stairs for more gossip.

BRAP!

ONE AFTERNOON at Khun Supaporn's, a bird flew into the house. It came through the open door, just as Nong and Oi had.

But the bird was confused. It tried to fly out through a window. BRAP! went its head against the pane.

Nong got up and opened the window. But the bird flew away and hit its head against a window on the opposite side of the house. BRAP! came the same sound again. The windowpane rattled in its slot.

Birds often flew into Nong and Oi's house. And they flew through the classrooms at school. But the windows at home and the windows at school had no glass. The birds that flew in could pass freely. They could stay for a visit, then go on their way.

The bird at Khun Supaporn's house did not have that freedom. Nong tried to help it, but by now the bird was excited. It flew higher, to get away from Nong, and it flew into the dormer windows above the main windows. The dormers did not open at all.

"Why do people need windowpanes, anyway?" said Nong.

"It's the modern style." Oi watched the bird but kept ironing. That was her job, after all. "New houses all have them."

"Whoever invented them must not have liked birds." Nong watched as this bird flew across the room and again banged its head.

It steadied itself and then flew back. The flapping of its wings was surprisingly loud.

Finally Oi got up, and they were able to steer the bird back toward the door. It flew out cautiously and then soared away. Nong had never seen a bird fly faster.

"Well, that's a relief," she said.

"I wonder what that bird will say to its friends?" said Oi as she sat down to continue her ironing.

For a long time after that, Nong could not forget the sound of the bird banging into the pane. BRAP! It wasn't fair. How could a bird know about glass?

At school her teacher told them about nature. That teacher's favorite topics were posture and sitting up straight, but that day she talked about nature. She even stood in a different part of the classroom.

"Look at what happens when people and nature collide," she said. "Pollution. That's one thing. And litter. Trees disappear from the forests. Innocent animals might die."

The students sat listening intently. *Collide* was a new word for them.

One boy raised his hand. "If the trees disappear, is it still a forest?"

"Of course," said the teacher. "When you go home, isn't this still a school?"

Then Nong raised her hand. She was thinking about innocent animals. She told the story of the bird that flew into windowpanes.

"Excellent," said the teacher.

Then another girl told about beetles. She said that there was always a beetle swimming in the water jar when she went to take her bath in the morning. She scooped it out and poured it onto the concrete. The beetle aired out its wings and flew away. The next morning, a new beetle would be there.

A girl in the back said that she had found a snake curled around their family's toilet. She said that when her father tried to poke it with a stick, the snake leaped straight up in the air.

"Aw, that's nothing," said a boy who sat in the corner.

"But this snake had a scar on its mouth," said the girl.

After that the stories kept coming. Some students told about chickens. There were stories about buffaloes and oxen. One boy told about frogs that came into his house. They hopped across the floor until they came to a wall, and then they got rattled. They kept jumping up against the wall, going nowhere. The boy said he watched one frog for hours, until his mother came in and told him to take it outside, or she would cook up a pot of frog soup.

"Did the frog have a scar on its mouth?" asked the boy who sat in the corner.

The teacher had walked around to the opposite side of the room. "What can we learn from these stories?"

"Houses are dangerous," said someone.

"Beetles can swim."

"Frogs are stupid," said the boy in the corner.

Everybody laughed. But the teacher held up her hands.

"Think for a minute. Are frogs really so stupid? How can frogs know about walls?" She looked at the boy in the corner. "Suppose you got dumped in a swamp. Would you know which way to go? There would be no walls to guide you. Maybe the frogs there would laugh about you."

She let them think about that. They thought about walls and about what it would be like to get dumped.

As they were thinking, a dog appeared in the doorway. He stood with his tongue hanging out of his mouth.

"Do you want to come in?" said the teacher. "You can join our discussion about nature." The dog looked at her, then turned and went on down the hallway.

"All right," the teacher said softly. "It's time for recess."

They put on their shoes in the hallway and walked downstairs in an orderly line. The dog sat off to the side, watching. By the time they were outside, everyone had forgotten about swamps and beetles and houses. Recess was no time to think about nature.

But as Nong ran across the dusty football field, the sound of that bird came back to her. Suppose there were a wall on the field that she couldn't see? What if she went BRAP! too?

"You are thinking too much," she told herself. But she slowed down a little, just in case.

The English Book

STARTING FIFTH GRADE not only meant that Nong had to wash clothes. She also began studying English. She learned to sing "The Alphabet Song" and to write all twenty-six letters—capitals first, and then lower case. She traced them all in her workbook while Oi was ironing at Khun Supaporn's house across the canal.

"I wish I had more books about English," Nong was saying. "I saw a lot of them at Serm-Thai." Serm-Thai was the name of the department store downtown.

Oi went on ironing. She had a big basket that she had to work her way through.

"Why does this family have so many clothes?" Nong asked.

Oi positioned one of Khun Supaporn's blouses on the ironing board. "They are important people. They have to change their clothes often. And keep your voice down."

"I never change my clothes. Just once a day, after school."

"You see? You're just a kid."

"It's the same as you." Nong was tracing the letter *Q* in her workbook. She liked making the soft round circle, then adding the slash firmly. It was a bit like her life. She went along happily for a while, and then hardness came up out of nowhere. She pressed down on the slash.

Khun Supaporn came into the room. "I have to go out now," she said. "Can I trust you? I keep asking myself that." She stood beside Oi, who was bent over the blouse seriously. "How old are you?"

"I'm seventeen."

"Seventeen? You don't look that old."

"I have big eyes. They make me look young."

"Hmm," said Khun Supaporn, whose own eyes were small. "I'm taking the key. When you finish, lock the front door, like this." She walked to the door. "See? I'm showing you how." She told Oi not to let anyone in the house and not to waste water if she went to the bathroom. Then Khun Supaporn went out to her car and drove off.

Nong closed her workbook and stood up. "Well, we're free."

"No, we aren't. We can't do anything. Especially not you. This isn't our house."

Nong went to the sofa and sat down. She tried to count the number of times in her life she had sat on a sofa. Then she looked through some magazines.

"I can read these," she said. She put one down and picked up another. She worked her way through the pile and picked up a book on the bottom. "This one's in English."

"You'd better put it back."

"I can read some. 'I.' Here's another one. 'I.' That's all I can read." Nong turned some pages. "It has pictures." This book was better than the one that Nong used at school. The pages were shiny and smooth. It had real photographs. It had more words, too, in smaller type.

An idea came to Nong. "I think I'll go home," she said. "Mom is there by herself."

She held the English book close to her side as she left. Oi went

27

on ironing. Nong hid the book in her schoolbag at home, and she showed it to her English teacher the next day.

"It's a beautiful book," said the teacher. "Just look at all these words. Do you mind if I keep it a while?"

Nong walked around the school proudly. The next day she went to the teacher and asked for the English book back.

"What do you mean?" said the teacher, whose eyes were small, like Khun Supaporn's. "I gave it back to you already." The teacher was sitting at her desk, checking homework. Nong had to crouch on the floor beside her, to make herself lower than the teacher.

"You borrowed it," said Nong. "You asked if you could keep it a while."

It was a daring thing for a student to disagree with a teacher. The teacher put down her pen. "I looked at that book, and then I gave it right back. You took it with you." She leaned toward Nong, though she kept her head high. "I want you to apologize for taking up so much of my time."

"But the book."

The teacher raised her eyebrows, and Nong hung her head. "I'm sorry," said Nong.

The teacher did not tell Nong that she had been so pleased with the new book that she had taken it to the principal.

"It's a beautiful book," the principal had said. "Do you mind if I keep it a while?"

That night Nong waited until she and Oi were in bed, under their mosquito nets, when the night seemed most peaceful. Then she told Oi what had happened.

"It isn't my fault. That teacher lied to me."

As usual, Oi remained quiet.

"Don't you believe me?" said Nong.

"Oh, I believe you. And maybe that teacher was wrong. But you

can't blame it on her. It's your fault for taking the book in the first place."

"I would have returned it. I just wanted to show it, that's all."

Oi stretched out on her mat. "Tomorrow you will have to tell Khun Supaporn."

"Why can't you tell her? I don't want to go back there."

The next day they walked through the front gate and up to the white cement house. Khun Supaporn brought out the clothes to be ironed.

"Remember to stay off the sofa," she told Nong.

But Nong was still standing beside her. "I have something to tell you," she said as Oi started in on the ironing. "Last week I borrowed one of your books, and now I can't find it."

"Is that so? Which book?"

"The one about English." Nong lifted the pile of magazines. "The one that was under all these."

"Oh. That one. Well, I wouldn't worry. You'll find it soon enough, and then you can bring it to me. All right?" She went out of the room.

Nong felt much better. Losing the book had been like a hard slash in her life.

But when Oi finished the ironing, Khun Supaporn brought in her pay and said, "You've done a good job. But you don't have to come back anymore."

Oi looked up at her. "Are you firing me?"

"Of course not. You're a wonderful worker. But, well, enough's enough."

"This is my fault," said Nong. "Please don't blame her."

Khun Supaporn smiled down at Oi. "I'm not angry. She's just a little girl. She doesn't know any better."

Oi stared at the money in her hands. "Thank you for giving me a chance."

"You're welcome," said Khun Supaporn. "Goodbye."

Nong and Oi had crossed the canal and were walking down the lane toward their home when suddenly Nong stopped. She looked back at the cement house. Khun Supaporn was in the doorway, watching them.

Nong spoke quietly. "I know better now," she said. She turned and walked the rest of the way home beside Oi.

The Policeman

SOMETIMES older boys came around to the house. They came delivering vegetables from market or asking Nong's mother if she needed some kind of help. But really they wanted to see Oi.

Oi was seventeen. She was pretty and a little bit shy. She had wide eyes that made her look young and innocent. This made the boys confident. When they saw her they began talking about themselves. Oi seemed to bring out their boasting.

"Which one of those boys do you like?" her mother asked one night as they ate leftover fish soup.

Oi shook her head as she dipped a ball of sticky rice into the broth.

Nong dipped her sticky rice into the broth, too. "Anyway," she said. "Which one?"

"I don't like any of them." Oi picked some bones from the fish. Leftover soup had more bones and less meat than first-day soup. In their house the leftovers were stretched out for days. Fresh water was added, and the broth grew thinner and thinner.

"Good," said Nong. "I don't like any of those guys, either."

But one of them was older than the others, and he had a job. He was a policeman. His motorcycle was much bigger than the boys' bicycles, and its engine made a deep, throbbing sound. The policeman's name was Yai.

Yai came around on Sunday afternoons. He sat downstairs with Oi on a low bamboo table. The downstairs of their house was one big room. Their father had built walls around the dirt floor. The walls kept out the sunlight and helped the dirt floor stay cool, even in summer.

Yai sat in the shadows of the big downstairs room. "What do you plan to do with your life?" he asked Oi one Sunday.

"I don't have any idea."

"Work? Study? What's your plan?" In his black boots and dark uniform, Yai looked even older than he was, and his words sounded even more serious.

Oi thought of that word: *plan*. She sat at the end of the table wearing sweatpants and a yellow T-shirt. "I'm still in high school. I haven't made any plans."

"Plans are important. I've planned my life, and, well, here I am now." He smiled at her. She was looking at the dirt floor. "She is shy," Yai was thinking.

"I have a plan for you, too," he went on. He looked around. "Where's your mother? I'd like to talk to her now."

Later, at dinner, Oi watched her mother and Nong eat from a bowl of bamboo-shoot soup. This broth was thick and gray from the fermented fish that gave it its flavor.

"What did he say?" she asked her mother.

"He's polite. He has a very sincere greeting."

Oi sat rolling a ball of sticky rice between her fingers.

"He made an offer," said her mother. "He said he would pay for your college education if you agree to marry him after you graduate." She said this casually. She chewed on a piece of bamboo shoot.

"What did you tell him?"

Her mother spooned up some gray broth. "I told him we'd talk."

Oi was still rolling the same ball of rice. "He wants to marry me?"

"He'll pay for your college."

"I thought so. He had a look in his eyes."

"He likes you. He said he'd come next week for your answer. I think he's sure you'll say yes."

That night, Nong and Oi lay upstairs in the darkness, under their mosquito nets. A motorcycle passed by. It slowed in front of their house, then went on down the lane.

"That was him," said Oi. "I know the sound of his motorcycle."

"Him who? You mean your husband?"

Oi sat up under the net. "He won't be my husband."

"He will. He wants to pay for your college." Nong was still lying down.

"I'll tell him I'm not going. Then I won't owe him anything."

"It won't work. He'll never let you say no."

The next Sunday, Yai came back looking more confident than ever. He let his motorcycle throb in the lane even longer than usual before he turned off the engine. His black boots had a fresh coat of polish. He kept his sunglasses on until he was standing in the dark downstairs of their house.

"Hello, Mom," he said to Oi's mother. "Here I am again, Oi."

"We talked a lot about your offer," said Oi's mother once they were all sitting down. "It's generous of you. But I have decided that Oi should finish high school before she thinks about offers like that."

Yai sat nodding. He leaned forward and smiled. "And then she will say yes?"

"I'm still in high school," Oi told him. "I haven't thought about anything yet."

Yai was still smiling. "I know. That's why I've thought about it all for you."

"Well, you know our decision," said Oi's mother. "If you're still interested when she finishes high school, you can come back again."

"Oh, I'll be interested. You'll still see me here every Sunday. Don't worry about that." Yai gave a confident laugh. "Well, thank you very much for your answer. Thank you very, very much." He was smiling directly at Oi.

When he left, he turned on his motorcycle and let the engine throb while he put on his sunglasses. He checked himself in one of the mirrors on his handlebars. Then he checked himself in the other. Finally he rode slowly down the lane. The slower he rode, the longer the throb seemed to linger.

Nong stood at the doorway watching him ride down the lane. Then she turned back to Oi. "He thinks you said yes!"

"Nong," said her mother.

"What are you going to do every Sunday? You can't be around when he comes."

"Nong," said her mother again.

"And what happens when you finish high school? What will you say to him then?"

"Something will come up," said Oi. "Something always comes up." Nong didn't know it, but that had been their father's philosophy.

Nong couldn't believe how calm Oi was being. She was about to speak up again, but her mother stopped her. "Nong. There are some dishes out back that need to be washed."

"I can wash them later. Oi, he thinks you love him!"

"Nong. Those dishes need to be washed right this instant."

Behind their house, Nong swished the dishwater around as quietly as possible. She knew that Oi needed her help. Oi, by herself, was no match for Yai, the confident policeman.

Nong rinsed the dishes, which had been used for leftover white-cabbage soup. She strained to hear what her mother was saying. But their voices were so soft that Nong could not even guess which one belonged to her mother, and which to Oi. Finally Nong forgot about the dishes completely and squatted by the back door, listening in.

But it was no use. Nong could hear nothing. She had to use her imagination to fill in the words of the conversation. Their mother, it turned out, was an expert at keeping her voice muffled.

It is something people learn by listening in all the time themselves.

Mosquito Nets

Nong and Oi slept on mats on the floor upstairs. They tucked their mosquito nets in around the edges of the mats, then lay looking out the window at the darkness, so black that it looked almost blue.

"Do people in those new cement houses use mosquito nets?" asked Nong one night.

Oi, who had been thinking about where she could go to earn money, answered slowly. "I guess not. They have windowpanes and screens."

"I'd rather keep the windows open," said Nong. "I'm glad we have nets."

They lay listening to the crickets and bullfrogs.

Nong rolled over to face Oi. "When you marry your boyfriend the policeman, will you sleep under a mosquito net? What if he buys you a big house with screens? What if he even has curtains?"

Oi rolled away from her, so that she was facing the wall.

Nong felt confident as she lay there. Mosquito nets had that effect on her. In the summer, when she slept outside on the balcony in order to let the cool breezes blow past, she crawled under the net and felt safe, even though she was outside the house. And inside, with the wooden house all around her, she could not fall asleep until she was under her net.

"How could a net make me feel safer than a house?" she had asked Mr. Pu late one morning. He was the old, shirtless man who lived down the lane. She told him a poem she had written about her mosquito net.

It is strong, though it is thin.

I feel safe when I crawl in.

Mr. Pu was the person who had introduced her to poetry, so Nong thought he would nod happily. Instead he said, "I bet I'm the only person you know of who doesn't use a mosquito net." He raised his bald eyebrows. "Want to know why?"

Nong had stopped at his house on her way back from riding alongside the canal, counting buffaloes. As usual, Mr. Pu had been sitting on the floor. He was holding a cup.

"Is it coconut cola?" Nong had asked him.

"Not today." Mr. Pu held up the cup. "This is tead ice." He sniffed the air twice, then again. "You smell thirsty. Like to try some?"

Nong had had tead ice before. Mr. Pu made it by freezing tea into ice cubes, then hurrying to eat them before they could melt. He explained that tead ice was something special, but once it melted it was only cold tea, which was hardly worth the trouble.

The woman who swept brought Nong her own cup of tead ice. Nong sat chewing it. "Why don't you use a mosquito net?" she asked Mr. Pu, for she knew he was an expert at not getting back to the subject.

"Ah. That. Well, there are two reasons. One has to do with my sister. The other has to do with my blood."

"What about it?" asked Nong as she sat cross-legged on his floor. "What's wrong with your blood?" Thinking about Mr. Pu's blood made her aware of her own, rushing around through her body.

"You don't know about blood? What do they teach you in school these days?" Mr. Pu put down his tead ice and held out his hands so that Nong could see his bare forearms. "See those veins? They've been in there a long time." He leaned down closer to Nong. "If our blood had a race, whose would win?"

Nong looked at the old veins.

"Yours would," he told her. "The blood you have is young and fresh. It's sprightly. But the older you get, the slower your blood moves. It gets tired in there. I'm so old now that my blood is too lazy to bleed."

"You mean if you cut yourself, your blood won't come out?"

"I'll show you." Mr. Pu looked around. "Over there on the table. I can use that pin."

Nong brought it over. Mr. Pu held the pin in the flame of a match for a moment. "Even old people have to watch out for germs," he said. Then he held the pin over the tip of his left thumb. "This is what they used to call 'science,' " he told Nong, and he pricked himself with the pin.

They watched the spot where the pin had gone in. At first there was just a tiny hole in the skin. Slowly some redness emerged. It came out stiffly, like a small thorn, before spreading tiredly over the thumb. Then it gave up.

"You see? What mosquito would want to eat blood as old and slow as that?" said Mr. Pu. "Should we try you?"

Nong pulled her hands back.

"For comparison," he said. "That's when the real learning comes."

Nong shook her head and held her hands behind her back.

Mr. Pu nodded. "You can try it yourself sometime. Your blood will rush out of you in no time. It's young. It hasn't learned yet." He put the pin on the floor. "Besides, your skin is too thin. It's easy for a mosquito to bite through." He smiled at her. "But look at mine." He held out his hands again. "See how tough my skin is? When I pull it, it stays up. Look at that."

He pulled up some skin on his hand. It sank back very slowly. He held out his hand toward Nong.

"Like to try it?"

"I want to hear the story about your sister."

"Ah, yes. That's one of my favorites." Mr. Pu put his hands, with their tired blood, down on his knees. "It happened one time when my sister and I were both young. But I had these very same veins in my hands already, even back then. One night she forgot to make sure her mosquito net was hung securely when she went to bed. That night it fell down on her. She rolled around in her sleep, and the mosquito net got wound tighter and tighter around her. It was so tight that it became a cocoon for my sister. The next morning, when we unwound the net, we couldn't find her. All we could see was a butterfly, wearing my sister's pajamas."

Nong, who was sitting with her knees pulled up to her chest, put her head back in laughter.

"Why, you don't believe me," said Mr. Pu.

Nong went on laughing. "I'm picturing a butterfly wearing pajamas."

"Don't forget, it was a special butterfly." Mr. Pu looked hurt. "Ever since then, I've been afraid of mosquito nets."

Nong was still laughing when she stood up. She finished her tead ice, then took a step toward the doorway. Mr. Pu was studying the veins in his hands. Nong turned and went back to him. She knelt down and took one of his hands in hers. She patted the stiff, spotty skin.

"Tough stuff, isn't it," said Mr. Pu. "But it keeps mosquitoes out."

That night, as Nong lay under her mosquito net, she did not feel as confident as she usually did. She rolled over on her side and asked Oi if a little girl could possibly turn into a butterfly, if her mosquito net fell on her, and if it were wound tightly enough around her.

Again Oi answered slowly. "Well, it never happened to me."

On those nights, with the windows open, and with the blood rushing around in her veins, everything seemed possible to Nong. She waited until Oi fell asleep. Then she got up and made sure both of their nets were hung securely, and she crawled back in with confidence.

The Buffalo Woman

ONE EVENING not long after that, when the Buffalo Woman came down the lane past their house, Nong got up and walked with her. The Buffalo Woman held a rope that was tied to a bell that hung from the buffalo's neck. The bell was wooden. As Nong and the woman followed the buffalo, the rope sagged. It was slow going.

Nong watched the buffalo's round body sway. She wondered what it would be like to have so much of yourself trailing behind you.

"Did you ever want to do anything else besides this?" said Nong, who watched the Buffalo Woman pass their house every day.

"Besides what?" said the Buffalo Woman.

"Besides taking care of buffaloes."

The three of them walked down the lane toward the *somtam* stand. The buffalo made the most noise. Its hooves clomped down in the sandy soil. And the wooden bell thudded dully. It sounded musical, though.

"No," said the Buffalo Woman. "I never did."

"Really?" Nong was trying to step in the buffalo's hoofprints.

"You always loved buffaloes?" She was eleven already and had no idea what she could do. She was not even sure if she knew what she loved.

"Well, maybe there was one other thing." The Buffalo Woman laughed. "It's hardly worth mentioning."

Nong was waiting to listen. But just then they came to the *somtam* stand, where Aunt Ray was cleaning up.

"Sold out?" called the Buffalo Woman.

"Sold out." Aunt Ray smiled as she scrubbed the mortar and pestle that she used to pound chilies. "Another good day."

Nong and the Buffalo Woman turned down the next lane, away from the main road. The buffalo led, and they followed.

"That's what I like," said the Buffalo Woman. "I like people. I like people and buffaloes."

Nong listened to the sounds of their feet. She was still waiting for the story. The buffalo's hooves sounded heavy, and the Buffalo Woman's sandals scraped along. Nong heard her own short steps mixing in. It was a good pace for talking.

"Please tell me," she said.

"Tell you what?"

"What you used to do."

"You want to hear that?" They stopped while the buffalo chewed on some grass. "A long time ago," said the Buffalo Woman, "I used to make sweets. The kind with sticky rice and coconut cream. I tried selling them. I took them to Aunt Ray's stand and sold them to people who bought *somtam*."

"Why did you stop?" asked Nong, who had often wished that there were sweets for sale at Aunt Ray's.

"Making sweets is hard work. But that isn't why. I still make them now, to give out for free."

The buffalo raised its head and went on down the lane. They followed.

"It was because I was always off to the side. People didn't go to see me. They went there to buy *somtam*. I was just an afterthought."

"An afterthought," said Nong.

"That's right," said the Buffalo Woman. "How did we get onto that?" A motorcycle passed, and she tugged the buffalo toward the side of the road.

"I think I'm an afterthought," said Nong. "In my family, I mean. I always feel like I'm off to the side." Nong surprised herself with her words. She had never known she had those feelings.

"But you're a child. Children are always smack in the middle."

"Not in my house. Everybody comes to see my mother or my sister. Nobody comes to see me."

"I don't believe that," said the Buffalo Woman. "I know your mother. I don't believe that for a minute."

Nong walked along silently.

"I'll come to see you," the Buffalo Woman went on. "I'll come every day. Do you want me to? I'll bring homemade sweets, just for you."

Nong could feel her face turning red. "That's all right. You don't have to. I was only complaining."

"You were feeling sorry for yourself."

"Yes."

"That's not a good habit. Complaining makes your skin become brittle, you know."

"I know," said Nong, though she didn't.

"Feeling sorry for yourself makes you lose all your friends."

Nong felt her ears burn with shame.

"And it makes your ears burn," said the Buffalo Woman.

Nong was looking down at her feet. "I'm sorry I said anything."

She felt a hand on her shoulder. The Buffalo Woman leaned down and lowered her voice. "If you think you're off to the side," she whispered, "how do you think the buffalo feels?" She raised her eyebrows at Nong and patted her shoulder. "You don't hear him complaining."

Nong looked ahead at the well-behaved buffalo. "I wasn't thinking," she said quietly. Out loud she said, "Please come. Please come to see me. And please bring the buffalo, too."

"His name is Coconut."

Coconut's bell thudded out, and his hooves clomped along in percussion. He stopped to sniff some bamboo.

"I'm sorry I said anything," said Nong.

"About what?" said the Buffalo Woman.

The Different Boy

ONE OF THE BOYS was different. He was the same age as Nong, but he played rough. When he joined in, fights began, and someone went home crying. Sometimes that person was Nong.

The Different Boy lived in a house by the buffaloes' field, apart from the rest of the village. That house was wooden and old. The interesting thing about it was that there was a large stuffed bear on the roof. One day, a few years earlier, the Different Boy's father had gotten angry with him, and had grabbed the bear, which was the Different Boy's only toy. The father had stomped out of the house and thrown the bear up on the roof. It lay in the rain and the heat, looking cheerful.

Everyone knew the story of the Roof Bear.

Now it was Saturday morning. One of Nong's friends, named Lek, had gotten a handful of firecrackers. They were not powerful. They looked like pieces of garlic, and when they were thrown down, they made a bang like a cap pistol. Though they were not all that loud, it was fun to catch people off-guard when the garlic went POP!

Nong and Lek went to the corner. They tried to sneak one of the exploding garlics into Aunt Ray's mortar as she was pounding her *somtam*. What a start that would give her! But Aunt Ray had too much experience with garlic. She picked out the fake one in no time. In fact, she threw it back at the girls, and it went off at their feet.

"Ha, ha, a-ha," laughed Aunt Ray, who had been young once herself.

Other kids joined Nong and Lek. They had heard the bang of the garlic and come running. Their whole group was up near the main road, ready to throw the garlic at the tires of motorcycles that passed, when they saw the Different Boy. He was coming toward them with his jaw stuck out. He swung his arms as he walked.

"Guess what I've got," he said.

"We're playing with garlic," said Lek. She made as if to throw one at his feet.

"Look." The Different Boy held his arm out in front of them. On his wrist was a shiny gold watch. "It's mine."

One of the boys gave a laugh. It was easy to see why. The watch was bright and sparkling, but the Different Boy's clothes were dusty and old. Even the seat of his pants was torn; everyone could see that he was not wearing underwear.

But the Different Boy was so used to his clothes that he did not notice the contrast they made with the watch.

"I'll let you wear it if you give me your garlic," he said.

"No," they said.

"Well, then I'll let you wear it for free."

They all tried it on. It was too big for their skinny wrists.

"Come on," said the Different Boy. "I'll show you where I found it." He led them down a lane to the canal. "Over there by the bridge." He stood back proudly and held the watch up to his ear.

"You should tell the police," said the boy who had laughed.

The Different Boy shook his head. "Finders, keepers."

"Well, you should at least tell your father."

The group nodded. "We'll tell him for you!" they shouted. They were ready to run to the Different Boy's house.

Then Nong spoke up. "You go tell his father. I'm going to look for more watches." She turned and ran down to the bridge.

Soon all of the kids were down there, looking through the weeds by the side of the canal. "I see one!" someone shouted, and they dove to that spot and found nothing. One time Lek stood back and threw a garlic at them. It was exciting, believing that the weeds contained watches.

"Look carefully," the Different Boy said. "There may be a matching gold ring." They all bent down lower.

That night, as Nong was at home eating bamboo-shoot soup, a great shouting rose up. The Different Boy's father was yelling, and the sound carried out through the village.

"Now what?" said Nong's mother.

Nong spooned up the gray soup. "He stole a watch. He said he found it in the weeds."

"Well, try not to listen," said her mother.

But the shouting was interrupted by a WHAP! as the Different Boy was spanked by his father. WHAP! WHAP! "Don't hit me," the Different Boy cried. "Please, don't!" But his father, a shirtless man with tattoos, spanked him again.

CRACK! came the sound as it carried up through the village to Nong.

The father kept shouting. "I'll throw you on the roof, too!" Then CRACK!

Nong reached out to spoon up more soup. Her mother took hold of her wrist, right where Nong had tried on the shiny gold watch.

"I want you to go play with him tomorrow," she told Nong.

Nong was picturing the Different Boy being thrown on the roof. Now that would be something.

"I think all of us will," she said as she spooned up more of the soup.

The Mystery Key

NONG'S FRIEND LEK lived across the lane. Lek was younger than Nong, so Lek called Nong "PiNong." This sounded funny to them. "Nong" is a word that means "younger sister," and "Pi" means "older sister." So the name that Lek called Nong meant "older younger sister."

It sounded funny, but it was polite. Nong called Lek "NongLek." It meant "younger sister Lek."

They were not really sisters. But Nong did not have a younger sister, and Lek did not have an older sister. So they were satisfied being sisterlike friends, using their sisterlike names.

Lek was a collector. She saved used stamps and matches and red rubber bands and kept them in old plastic bags. She collected the plastic bags, too.

If it was free, Lek kept it.

Collecting made sense to Nong. It seemed to her that Lek was doing something useful with her life.

Nong decided to become a collector.

The problem was deciding what to collect. Lek was already saving most of the good stuff—and Nong didn't want to imitate Lek. She went to her mother for advice.

"We don't have much worth collecting," said her mother. "You could collect old chili seeds, or caps off the bottles of fish sauce." She looked around for ideas. "There are all kinds of tree leaves out back."

Nong tried picking up leaves for a minute. Then she grew bored.

"Of course, some people aren't cut out for collecting," said her mother.

Another time Nong went down to Aunt Ray, who was not really her aunt, just as Lek was not really her sister. Nong had often seen Aunt Ray as she sat on her table making *somtam*. Aunt Ray always sat cross-legged. She seemed to know something about life.

"I've always been partial to garlic," said Aunt Ray. "But I guess that's not the kind of thing people collect." The pestle thump-thump-thumped against the mortar as her arms kept pounding the fresh papaya and sauce.

"I've known people who collected triangular pillows," said a woman who was waiting for *somtam*.

"And lottery tickets that ended in 9," said another.

"And anything shaped like a heart."

Neighbors were always coming around to Aunt Ray's. They shared their opinions while they waited for *somtam*. Then they went home to eat.

Aunt Ray herself took a taste of the fresh batch of *somtam*. "I would love to collect mortars and pestles," she said, "except that my old set might get jealous." She patted the mortar on the table in front of her, then leaned down and whispered to Nong. "I'm kind to my mortar. That's one of the secrets to making good *somtam*."

Aunt Ray sat back up and said, "Well, that doesn't help you much with your collection, does it?" She scooped the *somtam* into a plastic bag and tied it shut with a rubber band, which happened to be red.

Nong kept hunting for things to collect. One day she rode her bike down by the canal. It was hard work. The lane that ran alongside the canal was full of potholes and dogs. Nong had to ride along carefully.

Near the bridge where the boys sat fishing, Nong saw something metal in the dust of the road. It was a key. It was scratchy and dull. But Nong knew immediately that it was the start of her new collection. She put the key in her pocket.

She kept riding along. Now she was looking for keys. She had never had her own key before. Her house had no lock. None of the houses in her village had locks. There were no thieves in that village, and the houses had nothing worth stealing.

Nong felt the key in her pocket. She tried to imagine the door it would open. Maybe the door to one of the new cement houses. Maybe the door to a bank. Nong decided to take good care of her key.

Way down near the next village, Nong met the Different Boy. He was standing on the bank of the canal. Just as Aunt Ray was always sitting cross-legged, the Different Boy was always on foot.

"What are you doing?" Nong asked.

The Different Boy was under a tree. "I'm working on my collection."

"What collection?"

"Come here and see for yourself."

Nong laid down her bike and walked over.

"Here." The Different Boy pointed to the base of the tree.

"That's just an old shoe," said Nong.

"That's right. It's a part of my collection."

He led her along the canal bank to the next tree. By a stone at the base of the tree was a glove, as dirty and old as the shoe had been.

Nong looked confused.

"Don't you see?" The Different Boy shook his head, as if his time was always being wasted explaining. "What good is one shoe? What good is one glove?" He let it sink in. "I collect things that don't have their partners."

By the next tree was a chopstick. He led her on down the lane, where he showed her an eyeglasses lens and a pedal.

"Why do you keep everything here?" asked Nong. "Why don't you take it back home?" She was a little bit envious. It was a good idea for a collection—and a good place to keep it.

"I can't take things home. My father would throw everything up on the roof."

Nong thought for a moment. "I have something for your collection." She took the key from her pocket. "I don't have a lock to go with it."

The Different Boy looked the key over. "You know, I have a lock with no key."

He led her to a tree by a footbridge. He knelt down and pulled a lock out from behind a loose piece of bark. Then he brushed some dirt from the lock and tried the key in it.

The lock didn't open.

"It was worth a try," said Nong.

"I guess so. But I'm kind of glad it didn't work." The Different Boy stood up again. "It's not fair, you know. A key with no lock is a mystery. But a lock with no key is nothing at all."

They stood looking at each other. Then he gave back the mystery key.

✿ Part Two

Chicken Leaves

 ONE MORNING as Nong rode down the lane, Mr. Pu called out to her.

"Come in here a minute," he said. "There's someone I want you to meet."

This was during the time of the new water line. A lime stripe had been painted down the side of the lane to show workers where to dig the trench for the pipes. Up by the main road, construction had already begun. Some of the boys had climbed down and crawled through the new culvert. It would carry the water to their village, taking the place of their wells.

The boys found the culvert fascinating. Their faces became serious when they climbed down, as if playing underground were important in a way that Nong could not understand.

"Come on in," Mr. Pu repeated.

Nong had planned to ride along beside the canal and count buffaloes. But Mr. Pu had never called out to her before. She parked the bike and stood in the doorway. As usual, Mr. Pu sat on the floor with the checked cloth tied around his waist.

Beside him sat a much larger man in a shirt. His hair was white, too, like Mr. Pu's.

59

The men were looking at a plate on the floor in front of them.

"I want you to meet this man," said Mr. Pu. "He is my son."

"Mr. Pu is my son, too," said the man. Both of them gave a big laugh. Then the new man turned to Nong. "And who are you?"

"Ah, she is important," said Mr. Pu. "She's as important to me as the wheel is to the oxcart, as the blood is to the vein. Maybe more so."

"I am Nong."

"You see?" said Mr. Pu. "As young as that, yet she still has a name."

The other man nodded approvingly at Nong. "That's the stuff," he told her.

Nong sat down across from the men.

"My name is Pu," said the new old man.

Mr. Pu nodded. "We were named after each other."

The new man leaned down toward Nong. "He must like you. He makes sense when you're here."

Mr. Pu pointed to the plate. "I tell you that plate is empty."

The new man shook his head. "It can't be empty," he said, "because it hasn't been full yet. It's just a plate, that's all." He looked at Nong. "What do you think? Is this an empty plate, or is it just a plate?"

Nong studied the plate carefully. She noticed that the edges weren't chipped.

The new man leaned back. "Let me tell you my philosophy of life." He nodded importantly; then he checked to see if Nong was listening. "Some people are the blood," he said; "others are the veins. Some people are wheels, and others are oxcarts." He waited. "Well, I guess that's it."

Mr. Pu leaned in. "He used to be a cook. So his examples are always about food."

"That's right," said the new man.

"He just cooked this morning," said Mr. Pu. "It's a recipe I taught him back when we were both the same age."

"What is it?" asked Nong.

"Chicken leaves. Want to try some?"

The new man went into the back room and returned with another plate. It wasn't chipped, either. He put it down beside the first one.

"Chicken leaves," he announced.

"But those are wings," said Nong. "How can you say they are leaves?"

"It's a long story," said Mr. Pu.

The new man shook his head. "It can't be long," he said, "because it hasn't been short yet." He smiled at Nong; then he told her the story. "My doctor told me not to eat meat. But I love chicken. So I pretend it's a plant, and I eat it. Chicken leaves today, chicken stems tomorrow. I eat a vegetarian diet."

They all chewed on the chicken leaves and put the bones down in the first unchipped plate. Every time Nong picked up a leaf or put down a bone, she thought of the chips in the plates she ate from at home. Then a thought came to her.

"Aren't leaves supposed to be boneless?"

The new man stopped eating a moment, and he thought. "No," he said finally. "Leaves can't be boneless, because they never had bones to begin with." He gave a satisfied nod. "You see? Just promise you won't tell my doctor." He went back to eating.

Soon they had finished the chicken leaves. Mr. Pu pointed to the plate the leaves had been in. "Now that is an empty plate."

"Of course it is," said the new man. "But what about this one?" He picked up the plate where they had all put their bones.

"It's full now," said Mr. Pu.

But the new man was shaking his head. "It can't be full," he said, "because it was never empty. Remember?" He seemed very satisfied. "Besides, there's room for more bones here. So how can you say that it's full?"

"Because we're all out of bones," said Nong. "That plate is holding all of the bones that we have. So it is full."

The new man looked at her. "So you're on his side. Well, some people are." His voice had suddenly gone soft. "But some people aren't, I assure you."

"I'm not on anybody's side. I was just trying out my idea."

The new man squinted at her. "Have I told you my philosophy of life?"

But Nong excused herself and stood up. "I have to go home to my mother."

"That's it!" said the new man. "That is my philosophy of life!" He was excited again. He gripped Mr. Pu's arm. "Can you beat that?" He beamed at Nong. "I like the way that you think."

Mr. Pu turned toward Nong as she backed out the door. "Goodbye," he said.

The new man put his arm around Mr. Pu's shoulder. "It can't be good," he said, "because it hasn't been bad yet. Don't you see?"

Nong wheeled her bike into the lane and found that she was no longer interested in counting buffaloes. She rode up the lane and, keeping her promise, went back home to her mother.

Trenches

ONE OF OI'S EARLY-MORNING JOBS was to bring up water from the well in back of their house. She filled the big clay jar in the bathroom, and she brought up more buckets to fill the jar they kept for washing dishes and clothes. Soon that chore would be passed down to Nong.

Oi had learned not to complain about her work. Her mother could top all of her whining. "We had only one well for the whole village. We had to pull a cart full of jugs every morning and night. Do you know how heavy that cart was when the jugs were all full?" Her mother shook her head at the memory of her life's early troubles.

But Oi's job was about to become easier. One morning as she was bringing up buckets of water she heard men's voices at the end of the lane. They were digging a trench.

"For the new water pipe," one of the workers explained to Oi as she and Nong walked to school later. "It will take the place of your well."

Oi smiled at him. That made the worker feel confident. But Oi was not thinking about him. She was thinking about waking up in the morning and not having to get out of bed and lug water.

Trenches

That afternoon Nong came home before Oi and watched the men
dig the trench. They swung their hoes way up over their heads as they
worked. They brought their hoes down and lifted the soil out slowly.
They worked their way past Nong's house toward the canal. Their arms
were dark brown and muscular.

Watching the workmen made Nong think of Yai, the policeman.
He had come to see Oi for a while, but then he'd lost interest.

"You see?" their mother had told Oi. "He couldn't wait. Forget
about him. The last thing you need is an impatient husband."

The workmen were sweating and cheerful. Some of them talked
to Nong as they dug out the trench. "Where's your sister?" they asked.
"Which one of us does she like?" The workmen laughed and took
breaks in the shade.

The next morning they came back and filled in the trench. "We
dug it on the wrong side of the road!" They were laughing. "It's OK,
though. We get paid by the day."

They laughed again and walked off to begin the new trench.

That night it rained. Nong closed the shutters, but some of the
rain blew in through the cracks around the window frame. She used a
cloth to sop up the water.

"That's my job," said Oi as she lay under her mosquito net.

"I'm old enough," Nong answered.

It was true. The jobs that Oi had grown bored with were the same
ones that made Nong feel grown-up.

By the next morning, mud had washed into both of the trenches
in front of their house. Nong tried to step to the center of the lane, but
she sank down to her ankle. When she pulled her foot out, her shoe
stayed stuck in the mud.

"Guess we can't go to school," she said.

But their mother said, "Wait." She went around to the side of the house and returned with a board that was taller than she was. She laid it over the trench and said, "There."

That board had been their father's. He had been handy with wood. He would have been able to fix the leak at the window frame easily. His things were still by the side of the house.

"You can go to school now," said their mother.

Down the lane came the workmen. "Let it rain," they were saying as they scooped the mud out of the trench. "We get paid by the day." They smiled at Nong and her sister, who were careful to stay in the center of the lane.

Later that morning, Nong sat in school thinking. What if her teacher were paid by the day? Would she teach them the wrong thing one day, then come back and fix it the next? Could students be paid by the day, too?

In her mind, she kept seeing the board that lay over the trench in front of her house. She could picture her mother staring down at the board, thinking of Nong's father.

Nong told her teacher that she had a headache. At lunchtime she went home.

In the lane near her house were the workmen. Nong found the friendliest one squatting alongside some bushes. He was smoking a cigarette thoughtfully. A hoe was propped up beside him. The other workmen were carrying lengths of pipe down the lane.

"I wish I were a trench-digger," she told the squatting workman.

He held the cigarette up to his mouth. "Why is that?"

"I want to work hard. I want to get paid by the day."

The workman took his time inhaling the cigarette smoke. He was making his break last. "A day is a long time," he said. "Think of the things you could do in one day if you weren't digging trenches. Fishing. Living. Taking motorbike rides around town." Smoke puffed out of his mouth as he talked. "Just today I could have gone to the horse races."

"Those things aren't interesting. Working is interesting. Making things. That's what I want to do."

The workman looked at her blue-and-white uniform. "Why aren't you in school?"

"I told my teacher I had a headache."

"You shouldn't have done that. People who want to dig trenches aren't allowed to tell lies."

"Why not?" said Nong. "Who would know?"

"It's a strict rule. They teach us about it in trench-digging school."

"You went to trench-digging school?"

"Sure. I'm not allowed to lie, am I?"

Nong thought about that. "What happens to trench diggers who tell lies?"

The workman shrugged. "Some might get by for a while. Most of them end up without friends." He shook his head. "The guys I know are all honest. You see how cheerful they are? You can't be happy like that if you're lying. Liars have to spend all their time worrying if anyone's going to find out the truth."

He threw his cigarette butt into the trench and stood up. Nong watched his hands grip the hoe. "You can still get back to school if you hurry," said the workman. "Besides, by the time you get to trench-digging class, you just never know who your teacher might be."

He winked at her and went off down the lane for more work.

Rice Cakes

✿ IT WAS OI'S IDEA to sell *Kow Jee*, the grilled rice cakes dipped in a batter of eggs. She and Nong set up a table in front of their house. They grilled the rice cakes themselves and sold them to people who passed by. Usually one or two cakes at a time. People in their village did not have enough money to buy more.

Some people didn't buy any at all. They just stopped and talked. Passing by, neither buying nor saying anything, would have seemed harsh, at least on their lane.

"We don't make much," Oi said to Nong as they counted their earnings. "But even a little is something."

They were not the only family looking for ways to make money. Across the street, Nong's friend Lek and her mother sold boiled rice soup, with pieces of ground pork and onion. This soup was called *joke*. They woke up early and sat with a big pot of *joke*, waiting to make their own profit.

Lek's mother sold the soup in the morning. Nong and Oi sold the rice cakes after school, until dark.

"We spend all our profit on your soup," Oi said to Lek's mother.

"And we spend ours on your cakes," said Lek's mother. They laughed and went on with their selling.

Another woman down the lane who often bought both the soup and the cakes began selling grilled pork. She cut up the pork and skewered the pieces on sticks that she laid over hot coals.

Now the profits were divided three ways.

One day a young man stopped by and bought a rice cake. He said he was just out of college. "You ought to have a sign," he said. "I almost didn't see your stand."

"We don't really need one," said Nong.

"But you do. A sign can increase your profits." The young man finished his rice cake. "And I can make a sign for you."

"How much?" said Oi.

The young man stepped back from their stand. He looked up at their house behind them, then around at the lane. He thought for a moment in a businesslike way.

He named a price.

Oi laughed. "That's more than we make in a month." Nong laughed, too.

"But if you have a sign," said the young man, "you can make even more. That's my point."

Oi smiled at him. "No, thank you."

"I can make first-class signs."

She shook her head. "Sorry."

He shrugged his businesslike shoulders and climbed on his motorcycle.

"Don't forget to pay for your rice cake," said Nong.

They watched him ride down the lane and buy some grilled pork.

"He must think we're stupid," said Nong.

Oi shook her head. "He's just trying to do business."

"But we don't need signs. Anyone can see what we sell."

"People don't really need rice cakes, either. That's one thing to remember." They watched the young man ride away from the grilled-pork stand. "I feel sorry for him," said Oi.

"I don't," said Nong. "He should find a worthwhile way to make money." And she ate one of their rice cakes.

It was nearly dark when the Buffalo Woman passed with Coconut, her buffalo. She smiled at them and kept walking.

"I was going to give her a rice cake for free," said Nong after the Buffalo Woman had gone. She looked down the lane where the Buffalo Woman had disappeared. "Tomorrow I will," she decided.

But the next day the Buffalo Woman did not pass. Nor the day after that. Finally on Saturday Nong rode her old bicycle down to the buffaloes' field. The Buffalo Woman was in a corner, chopping some branches into kindling. Coconut was chewing on grass.

"I've been waiting for you to pass by," Nong said.

The Buffalo Woman kept chopping. "I go the back way now."

"By the canal? But that's too far!" Nong held out a bag. "Some rice cakes," she said.

The Buffalo Woman shook her head. "No, thank you."

"Two," said Nong. "One for you; one for Coconut."

"I didn't bring any money."

"They are free."

The Buffalo Woman gave Nong a long look across the weeds. "That's kind of you. But no, thank you."

"Will you go home past our house? I'll keep them warm for you." Nong came up close. The Buffalo Woman was looking away. "Are you all right?"

The Buffalo Woman stood up. "No, I'm not." Her voice was quiet but sure of itself. "I think it's cruel that you started selling those things. When I walk past your stand all I can think is that I'm so poor I can't even buy a rice cake."

Nong stared at her.

The Buffalo Woman went on. "There's no reason to sell unneces-
sary things. There's no need to be greedy." She came into the open and
stood in front of Nong. "Now I have to take the long way back home
every night. Think how I'd feel if I passed you."

Nong looked down at the bag of rice cakes in her hand. "We're
just trying to make money ourselves. We don't know what else to do."

"The world isn't fair," said the Buffalo Woman. "There's no need
for you to add to it." She reached out toward Nong and took the bag.
She crossed her arms angrily. Then she took out a rice cake. That made
her grow calmer.

"Well, that's all I wanted to say. Spending so much time with a
buffalo makes me a little bit anxious, you know."

71

"That's all right," said Nong.

The Buffalo Woman took a bite out of the cake. "It's been a long time since anybody gave me anything."

Nong watched her chewing. "Will you go home the old way now? Can you come past our stand?"

The Buffalo Woman swallowed. "I don't know. Not if you're going to give me rice cakes for free every day."

"Oh, we wouldn't. Just this once."

"Because I couldn't take that. I couldn't stand for that at all."

"We'd just say hi. We just want to see you and Coconut."

The Buffalo Woman held up the other rice cake. "Say. Do you think he'd mind if I ate his?"

Coconut was still chewing his grass. The Buffalo Woman looked at Nong. "Shhh," she said, and she ate the leftover rice cake.

Spigot

THE TRENCHES WERE FINALLY FINISHED, and the water pipe was connected. It took a long time. Rain fell hard every night, and the workmen spent the mornings scooping out fresh mud so that they could get back to the pipeline. They scooped cheerfully, though. Then it rained hard again.

After the pipeline was finished, a man came around with a notice. "Please conserve water," it said. He gave it to Nong's mother.

"How can we conserve it when we don't have any to begin with?" She took the man around to the back of the house and turned on a spigot the workmen had installed. It coughed and even gave a shiver that made the man jump away. But no water came out.

"Conservation is important," said the man, who was wearing a dark uniform. "Did you know that the Chee River is two inches lower than last year at this time? If that keeps up, next year it will be lower yet."

"We're doing our part," said Nong's mother, and she turned off the spigot, which had begun to shake violently.

The man turned to Nong. "Do you study conservation in school? Do they teach you that humans waste more water than almost any other animal?" He shook his head. "If I was your teacher, you wouldn't need people like me to come around and tell you." He walked off with his packet of notices.

Every day Nong and her mother turned on the spigot. And every day nothing came out.

Then after a month the same man came back. He rode a motorcycle and wore a pair of dark glasses.

"Water bill," he said. He held out a slip of paper.

"But we still don't have any water," said Nong's mother.

"You're connected," said the man. "There's a monthly user's fee."

"But we didn't use any."

"Well, you have to pay, or you'll be disconnected."

"Let us be disconnected then," said Nong's mother. "I've been disconnected all my life."

"Me, too," said Nong.

The man pulled out a notebook. He unfolded a chart marked "Regulations."

"Hmm," he said. "Can you prove you haven't used any water this month?"

"Of course not."

The man smiled at her. "Yes, you can." He got off the motorcycle and walked along the pipeline until he came to a jasmine bush. He lifted up a branch. "Here is your meter," he said proudly.

The man knelt down. "This meter's stuck on zero. You must have broken it." He looked back at Nong. "Were you playing with this meter?"

Nong and her mother stared at him.

The man got up. "Don't worry. I'll have a repairman come out and check it for you." He held out the bill again. "It's due by the end of the month. Or the city will fine you for making a late payment."

"What if we'd rather be disconnected?"

"There's a disconnection charge. I think the city just raised it."

That night Nong finished washing the dishes with well water. She went over and turned on the spigot. It coughed and shook, as usual. Then it made a new sound. A trickle of water came out.

"Hey, everybody," said Nong. She put a freshly washed bowl under the spigot.

Her mother and sister came out. The three of them stood watching the bowl fill with water.

"That's a first for this house," said Nong's mother.

But something was wrong.

"That water's yellow," said Nong.

"It's red," said her mother.

"It's rusty," said Oi.

Nong dumped the water out and collected a new bowlful. But it was red, too.

"I can't wash my face with that," said Oi.

"Or brush my teeth," added Nong. She and Oi both made faces. Nong imagined the dirty water washing over her tongue. She turned away and spat out some saliva. Her mother did not even scold her.

"That's enough," she said. "Turn it off."

They tried the spigot every day. The water was still dirty.

The same man came around a month later with the next bill. He gave a smile.

"I'm glad you changed your mind about disconnecting," he said. "Our goal is to satisfy customers."

"Come look at this," said Nong's mother.

They went around back and turned on the spigot. Out came the reddish trickle.

"Not very powerful, is it?" said the man. He looked down at Nong. "Have you been playing with this spigot?"

Nong's mother put her hands on her hips. "The water is red!"

"Oh, that," said the man, and he gave a laugh. "That's common. The pipes get clogged up, and you have to clear them. Just let the water run for a while." He looked very satisfied with his answer.

"What about conservation?" Nong asked him.

"That comes later. Service always comes first." He held out the bill. "If you pay me now, you can save yourself a trip to the office."

"Well, I'd rather go there," said Nong's mother. "I want to file a complaint."

"Complaints must be filed through me."

"Through you?"

"That's right. I'm your water-services agent." He stood a little bit straighter and took a sheet from his notebook.

"Now," he said. "What seems to be your problem?"

Behind him, the spigot coughed and went dry.

The Bottles and
Newspaper Woman

✿ IN NONG'S VILLAGE, the rules of behavior were clear. Children got haircuts and went to school. Women washed dishes and cooked. Men drank whisky and smoked. And older women chewed betel.

Betel was a nut that turned the women's teeth red. It turned their gums black. Nong never thought to ask why only the older women chewed betel. It was a fact of life in their village, like blue skies, brown houses, and red dust.

One woman who chewed betel was the Bottles and Newspaper Woman. She pushed a cart up and down the lanes of their village, hauling away people's stuff. She took only the things that she could sell at the junkyard. At the junkyard, she emptied her cart and pushed back home with a profit.

Just by listening, it was easy to tell how much stuff she had gotten. The emptier her cart, the louder it rumbled as she went down the lane.

The Bottles and Newspaper Woman had a technique for making

77

people give her their stuff. She pushed her cart up in front of a house and then waited. After a while she called out.

"Any paper?" she called. "Any bottles? I need money to buy rice. Oh, please, can't you help me?" She had a way of moaning as she spoke. Even her voice seemed to ache.

Most people gave her something. Keeping an old woman from starvation made them feel good about themselves.

One Saturday she pushed her cart up in front of Nong's house. Nong was inside, sitting on the bamboo table, reading a comic book. It was the only comic book she had, and she had read it many times before. It was always satisfying to see the story come out the same way again.

Nong saw the Bottles and Newspaper Woman out front. Then she went on reading.

She had read several more pages before the woman's voice rose up. "Any paper? Any bottles?" There was a pause, and she went on with her speech.

Nong got up and went out to her. "We don't have anything," she said.

"Just some old paper. Just some old bottles."

Nong shook her head. "We never have anything extra."

"How about that book?"

Nong held up the comic book. "This one? I'm reading it."

"It's dog-eared," said the Bottles and Newspaper Woman. "I could sell it for money to eat with."

"But it's mine." Nong felt strange refusing something to someone so much older than she was.

The woman laughed. "I give up food so that you can read. These are the sacrifices I make. What would your mother say about that?" She walked over to the side of their house and spat out the

juice from her betel onto a papaya tree. The thick red saliva ran down its trunk.

"What's this stuff?" asked the Bottles and Newspaper Woman. She was pointing back alongside the house.

Nong went over. "It's wood."

"It's scraps," said the woman. "You don't have any use for them." She looked through the pieces of wood.

Nong stood by the Bottles and Newspaper Woman's cart and watched her. The sides of the cart were made of pieces of cardboard that the woman had lashed together with plastic string. Hung over one side was a wire basket with a jug of water and a cup. Inside the cart were some more pieces of cardboard, weighted down by some old dusty bottles.

The cart was nearly empty.

"I can sell this wood," said the woman. "I can give you some money for it."

Nong shook her head. "I'm not allowed to get rid of it."

"But you can't use it. If you let me take it, we'll both get some money. Don't be a silly little girl."

"That wood is my father's," said Nong.

"What will he use it for?"

"He is dead."

"He wouldn't have wanted an old woman to starve, would he?"

"My mother wants to keep this wood here. She told us we shouldn't even touch it."

The woman pulled out a piece of the wood. "Let me tell you about my life. Every day I get a little bit here, a little bit there. At the end of the day it adds up to enough. But if I keep getting nothing—nothing here, nothing there—at the end of the day I still have nothing."

Nong was watching the saliva run down the papaya tree trunk.

80

"Just a few pieces," said the woman. "For my rice."

Nong went over by the wood. In back of the pile were some planks that were almost hidden.

"Yes," said the woman. "Those."

Nong shook her head. "I'm not allowed to. You'll have to wait till my mother gets back from the market."

"But she will say no."

"That's right."

"And then I will starve. Just give me one piece, from the back."

"It's wrong."

"It's worse if you don't. If you help me starve, it's a sin."

"It's a sin to disobey my mother."

"You will sin either way. So the least you can do is help me." The woman smiled, showing her betel-red teeth.

Nong looked away from that mouth. She could feel the red smile remaining.

"Maybe one piece," she said.

The woman's smile grew wider. Her black gums showed clearly. She pulled out two of the planks and placed them in her cart, moving the bottles off to one side.

"One more?" she asked. Nong stood aside as the woman pulled another plank out of the pile.

"I'm not being greedy," said the woman as she put the third plank in with the others. "We all have to get by." She reached into a plastic bag tied to the cart and took out some coins. She gave them to Nong. "For the wood."

Nong held the money flat in her palm.

"Buy anything you want," said the woman. "Reward yourself for such a good deed." She spat out more red saliva and went on down the lane. The wood rumbled loudly in her cart.

Nong was looking down at the coins. They felt dirty. How could she explain them to her mother?

Next door, the Bottles and Newspaper Woman was waiting. "Any bottles?" she called out to the house. "Any wood? Oh, please, help an old woman get through her life!"

Scorpions

NONG HAD BEEN IN SCHOOL long enough to know that every teacher had one or two points to harp on. With one teacher it had been posture; she went around the room with a ruler, cracking the forearms of students who rested their chins in their hands. "Sit straight," that teacher commanded. "Heads high! Arms in the ready position!" She stopped teaching the lesson for minutes at a time to make sure that her class was sitting properly enough to listen.

Another teacher's sticking point was handwriting. She was an older woman who taught them that oddnesses in their handwriting were caused by weaknesses in their personalities. She wanted every student's handwriting to be exactly the same.

"Careful—you're revealing yourself," she cautioned, and they sweated.

Once she pulled Nong aside and pointed out an *o* that Nong hadn't quite closed.

"What's wrong?" asked the teacher. "Are you having problems at home?"

Nong's newest teacher was a man. He did not take an interest in handwriting or posture. Instead, he warned the students about scorpions.

"Their sting brings on terrible pain," he told them on the first day of school. And then he said, "Their sting brings on terrible pain."

Nong had never seen a scorpion at that school, but she had never had a male teacher, either, so she sat forward and listened. Her arms were in the ready position.

"I was stung when I was your age," said the male teacher. "One day I reached into my schoolbag to get out my math book, when POW! That's when the scorpion got me. He was hiding in my schoolbag!" The teacher looked around the room with wide-open eyes. "The pain shot through my hand and all the way up to my shoulder. I made up my mind then that I would become a teacher so that I could warn all of my students about the dangers of scorpions. And now here I am." He stopped suddenly. "It was in my schoolbag!" he repeated.

That teacher led them out to the hallway. The rules of the school said that the students had to take off their shoes and put them in a row in the hallway before they went into the classroom. They studied in their stockings, which often had holes.

"Look at these shoes," said the teacher. "Scorpions love shoes. They like to crawl up into the toes of the shoes where it's dark and cool. Fifty-two students, 104 shoes. That's 104 hiding places for scorpions." He shook his finger at the students. "If I ever see any of you putting on your shoes without checking for scorpions first, I'll give you a crack with this ruler!" He showed them a ruler even bigger than the one the posture teacher had used.

"Time for recess," he said.

He stood and watched as they looked carefully into their shoes, all the way up to the toes. His ruler was in the ready position. Even after checking, the students put their shoes on cautiously, and some of them winced as they slipped their feet in.

Scorpions

"We lucked out today," said the teacher, after none of the students had been stung.

Scorpions kept coming up in his teaching. "Suppose Boy A has ten scorpions," he'd ask them in math class, "and he gives half of them to Boy B. How many scorpions will they have altogether?"

Another time, a bird flew into their classroom. "The best thing about birds," he said, "is that scorpions can't fly."

One time he called on Nong. "How many scorpions in a dozen?" he asked her. "Why did the scorpion not cross the road?"

Nong found herself wondering where all the scorpions were hiding, even after she had gone home from school. She looked at all the dark places—her father's woodpile, the corners downstairs—that she had never thought about before. Suddenly she imagined them being full of scorpions, with nothing to do in their lives but wait in the darkness to sting her. She began to sit scrunched up, with her legs tucked underneath her, so that no part of her body was too far away from her eyes.

Her teacher told new scorpion stories. "I've known scorpions that hid in the folds of floor mops," he said. "How many of you have floors? I knew a scorpion that hid in a pair of my best friend's pants. How many of you have friends? How many of you have ever worn pants?" The teacher was leaning out toward them as he spoke.

"It's time for art class," he went on. "Draw anything today but a scorpion."

Nong and her friends felt their days being filled up by scorpions. They walked to school looking down; their eyes were keeping a lookout. They scouted out rooms from the doorway before they went in. At recess, when a ball rolled into some bushes, no one dared reach in to get it. It may still be in there.

85

Only one boy was different. That was the Different Boy. "Some of my best friends are scorpions," he told them. "My father says being stung by a scorpion is what makes you into a man. He's been stung plenty of times. He lets scorpions run loose in the house, just to toughen himself up."

"Oh, yeah?" said someone. "Let's go and see them."

"Well, they used to be there," the Different Boy said. "But the police made him take them away."

For all of their talk about scorpions, no one was stung. One boy said he found one in his bathroom at home, but his grandmother mashed it to death with a garden hoe. He said it's not a sin to kill a scorpion if you've ever been stung by one, as his grandmother had.

"It's a relief to me that no one's been stung," said their teacher. "That shows you how effective my teaching has been."

But some of them became more and more curious. How much pain could a little bug cause?

One night at home, Nong's mother was cooking white-cabbage soup.

Nong sat and watched her. "Why don't we ever eat scorpion?"

"No one does that. What's wrong with white cabbage?"

Nong didn't answer. She was thinking that white cabbage was dull. The soup barely gave off an aroma.

"Nothing ever happens to me," she said.

Her mother was stirring the soup. "What would you want to have happen? You're still a young girl, remember. Things shouldn't happen to girls."

"I want to get stung by a scorpion."

"No, you don't."

"I want to know what it's like."

"Why don't you burn yourself, then?" said her mother. "Do you know what that's like? Why don't you sleep with red ants? Why don't you lie down under a buffalo?" She was stirring the soup with more vigor.

"What if I become a teacher?" said Nong. "I won't have anything to teach my students. If they ask me what it's like to be stung by a scorpion, I'll have to say I don't know. How can they learn anything that way?"

But later, when Nong went upstairs to bed, with a stomach full of white-cabbage soup, she stepped carefully and avoided cracks in the floor where scorpions may have been hiding. She shook out her pajamas. She even checked under her pillow.

Nong crawled under her mosquito net cautiously. She winced a little as she lay back. Then at last she closed her eyes.

Darkness. Cool darkness.

A perfect hiding place for scorpions.

The Doctor

WHEN SOME CHILDREN GET SICK, they complain a lot and claim that they can't go to school. Some children do that even when they are not sick at all.

But Nong was different. When she got sick, she said nothing. She did everything with more energy than usual, so that she would make up for her body's weakness. At night she slept as hard as she could in order to feel better the next day.

There was a reason for that. If Nong's mother knew that Nong was sick, she would insist on telling the doctor. Doctors cost money; Nong's family was poor. So Nong hid her symptoms and tried her best to be strong. She did not want to cost her family any more than she had to.

One night she felt a fever coming on. She lay sweating under her mosquito net until morning. She took deep breaths and put on her uniform for school.

"Goodbye, Mom," she said as powerfully as she could.

But her mother had been a mother for many years, and she could spot symptoms as easily as she could slice cabbage.

"What's wrong?" she said. "Your face is all red." She put her hand on Nong's burning-hot forehead.

Nong was sent back to bed.

Her mother went across the street to Lek's mother. "Please go tell Doctor Wichai that Nong is sick," she said. Then she came back and sat with concern beside Nong.

Doctor Wichai lived on the next lane and rode a bicycle with his medical kit in the basket up front. He wore blue, collarless shirts, like the farmers, and as he pedaled down the lanes of the village, he sang folk songs that carried out over the ricefields.

"If I were born as a cloud in the sky, I'd take shade to the farmers in the fields," he sang as he biked up to Nong's house that morning.

Nong was lying on a mat on the bamboo table downstairs.

"I don't know what happened," said Nong's mother. "This morning she—"

Doctor Wichai held up his hand. "Don't tell me," he said as he crossed the dirt floor. "Let me guess." He gave a smile. "Guessing illnesses is a hobby of mine. It's like a game. Being sick is a game, you know. I'll help you win." All this time, he was kneeling by Nong, looking her over.

"What is it?" he asked. "Old age? Sore hair?" He bent closer and said, "Hmm."

Nong's mother brought him a glass of cold water.

"I know what it is," Doctor Wichai said finally. He sat on the table beside Nong. "You've been having bad dreams."

Nong nodded weakly. "I've had dreams about scorpions and bad mangoes."

"It's those dreams," said the doctor. "They've zapped all your pep." He put his hand up to her forehead. "You're hot. You're hot enough for two little girls. Why do you want to hog all the fever?"

He turned to Nong's mother. "What day is this?"

"It's Monday."

"Ah," he said. "There's a cure then. Do you know Aunt Oom's Soup Shop? Ride my bicycle up there and order a bag of her Fever Buster soup. On second thought, I'll go myself. A sick little girl should stay with her mother."

He rode off, singing. He came back again with a plastic bag full of soup. It was in the basket with his medical kit.

"She should breathe in the aroma of the soup before she eats it. Make sure she breathes deeply. Serve it in a cream-colored bowl."

Doctor Wichai smiled at Nong. "Well, I guess that's it. You should feel better tomorrow at a quarter to ten in the morning." He turned and went out to his bicycle.

Nong's mother followed him. "How much?"

He shook his head. "For a cute girl like that? Who would much rather be healthy and off with her friends at school?" He shook his head again and swung his leg over the seat. "Remember to make sure she breathes deeply."

He rode off, singing, "If I were born as a grain of sand, I'd make a path for the masses." He hadn't even opened his medical kit.

Sure enough, Nong began to feel better the next day, although she forgot to check the time. And the day after that, she went back to school.

"There's something that bothers me," said her mother that evening as she cleaned the rice for their supper. "Doctor Wichai wouldn't take any money. But we can't let him come here and treat you for nothing." She turned to Nong. "Look. Here's a bag of mangoes. Ride over to Doctor Wichai's. Give him the mangoes as a way to say thanks."

Nong and Oi rode over on the bicycle that was too small for Oi's legs. Nong was still tired. She sat behind Oi. Sometimes she leaned forward and rested her head against Oi's back.

Doctor Wichai's bicycle was parked beside his house. It was facing the lane, as if to make it easier for him to ride out and treat the next patient.

When Oi called out for him, his wife came to the door.

"Doctor Wichai is taking a bath," she said. "Is something the matter?"

"No," said Nong. "Nothing's the matter. I was sick this week, and Doctor Wichai cured my fever. Here are some mangoes as a way to say thank you."

"That's very nice of you," said the doctor's wife as she took the bag. "He will appreciate that."

"He's a good doctor," said Nong. "Please tell him that Nong feels much better."

"He will be glad to hear it." The doctor's wife was smiling at them. "Thank you so much for the mangoes."

Nong and Oi stepped back to their bicycle. "Goodbye," they said. "They are for you, too."

The doctor's wife smiled again. As she opened the door to go in, Nong and Oi had a chance to look inside the house. There on a table were more bags of mangoes. A whole pile of bags. The mangoes were plump and looked juicy.

Nong and Oi rode off in silence. At the end of the lane, Nong said, "Did you see that?"

Nong felt Oi nodding. "Yes. I saw it."

They rode along. "Poor Doctor Wichai," said Nong.

When they got home, their mother said, "Well, did you give him the mangoes?"

They nodded.

"That was a special batch," said their mother. "I picked out the best ones. I'm sure he'll enjoy them."

Oi was looking down at the floor. Nong looked down, too.

Their mother was smiling. "Isn't it nice to do the right thing? Now let's eat." She went to the kitchen in back of the house.

Nong looked up at her sister.

"His whole house was full of them," she whispered.

"Well, I wouldn't go that far," said Oi.

The Soup Shop

❁ UP BY THE MAIN ROAD was a shop that sold bowls of steaming-hot soup. It opened onto the street. Out front stood a woman by a big copper pot, making bowl after bowl of the soup. Customers called out their orders as they got off their bicycles and walked in.

The woman laughed and said, "Coming up fresh in a minute!" Her voice carried off down the street; that attracted even more customers.

The woman's name was Aunt Oom, and the big copper pot she stood beside was full of broth. The name of her shop was Aunt Oom's, but most people called it the Copper Pot Shop.

Like most soupmakers, Aunt Oom was a red-faced woman with a laugh and busy, busy hands.

One day as Oi passed by Aunt Oom's on her way home from school she saw a "Help Wanted" sign out front, near the copper pot. Oi stopped in.

"Come by on Saturday morning," said Aunt Oom, whose hands were slicing very fresh pork.

At home, Oi told her mother that she'd gotten a job at Aunt Oom's.

"That's good news," said her mother. "What will you do there?"

"I didn't ask," said Oi.

"That's good. You don't want to seem fussy. How much will she pay you?"

"I didn't ask that, either."

"That's all right, too. You don't want to seem greedy."

On Saturday, Oi went off to work. It was just after sunrise.

Nong ran out of the house after her. "I'm coming with you," she said.

They walked up the lane and around the corner, toward the main road. Soon they arrived at Aunt Oom's.

"This is my sister," said Oi. "She came to help me."

"Well, get to work then," said Aunt Oom. "Wash these two bins of vegetables, and cut them this size." She held up her fingers. "Then slice this meat." She gave a laugh, and her hands, which for the moment had nothing to do, held each other tightly.

Nong and Oi squatted down in the room behind the shop and got to work. Aunt Oom was out front, bringing the broth to a boil. She stood by a counter where she kept her ingredients. Beside that was the big copper pot, over a charcoal fire. Inside the shop were eight or ten tables with stools.

Nong and Oi squatted there chopping. The sound of their knives against the cutting boards echoed in the small back room.

POK-POK-POK-POK-POK-POK-*POK*!   COPPER-COPPER-COP-PER-COPPER-COPPER-COPPER-*POT*!

That was the sound of their chopping.

"This job is all right so far," said Oi.

They took the vegetables and pork to Aunt Oom. "Now make sure the container of fish sauce on each table is full," she said. "The customers will come any minute."

Aunt Oom's had no menu. Everyone who ate there knew what

she served—noodle soup with fresh pork or meatballs. Nong and Oi carried the bowls to the customers, then cleared off the tables. It was not hard.

"This is fun," said Nong. "I like serving people. It seems like a polite thing to do."

"Here come some more customers," said Oi.

Many of the customers hunched down close to the bowls with the soup steaming into their faces. With chopsticks they raised big globs of noodles to their mouths and chewed steadily. When the bowl was empty, they reached out for a glass of cold water, and swallowed it all in a gulp. They sat giving satisfied nods. They talked to Aunt Oom for a while; then they paid up and left.

Nong noticed that the customers were smiling as they went out of the shop. She found herself following them to the front and watching as they headed toward the main road.

"Aunt Oom," she asked. "Why does your soup make the customers so happy?"

Aunt Oom smiled as she prepared a new bowl. "So you think there's something magic about it," she said.

"Yes," said Nong, who hadn't thought that at all, but liked the idea.

"Well, what do you think it is?"

Nong stood thinking. "It may be this copper pot. It's a big one. There must be something special about it."

"Oh, it's a powerful pot, all right. I couldn't make soup without it. But I don't think it's magic." She sent Nong to the back room again, this time to wash the bowls and the chopsticks and glasses.

Nong carried the freshly cleaned bowls to the front.

"You're a good worker," said Aunt Oom. She looked at the bowls. "How clean are they? Are they clean enough to hold magic?"

Just then two men came walking out past them.

"Great soup today," said one of the men.

"Even better than usual," said the other. "My stomach is singing."

"And mine's dancing!" said the first. They clomped away toward the main road.

Nong watched them leaving. "It must be the broth," she said to Aunt Oom. "People eat every last drop. Is that what makes them so happy?"

"Why don't you see for yourself?" And Aunt Oom made bowls of soup for Nong and Oi to eat in the back room.

"I wonder if my stomach will sing," said Nong as she slurped up the broth and the noodles. She made sure she ate every last drop.

"I wonder how much Aunt Oom will pay us," said Oi, who ate every drop, too.

After that Nong watched carefully as Aunt Oom made bowls of soup. She made every bowl fresh, mixing the broth and the pork and the bean sprouts. Then she added some spices.

"What's that?" asked Nong as Aunt Oom added a dash from a jar.

"Just some fish sauce."

Fish sauce wouldn't make your stomach sing.

Then Aunt Oom added a spoonful of something else.

"And that?"

Aunt Oom shook her head. "Only sugar."

Sugar wouldn't make your stomach dance.

Then Aunt Oom reached under the counter. She pulled out a bright red bottle and raised her eyebrows at Nong.

"Don't tell anybody." To a new bowl of soup, she added a single drop from the bottle. The drop fell so quickly that Nong was not even sure she had seen it.

"There," said Aunt Oom. "Now you know."

"What is it?"

Aunt Oom leaned down and whispered. "It's the Secret Sauce."

"Secret Sauce?" Nong's eyes had opened wide when her ears heard the word *secret*.

"That's right. I'm not even allowed to tell you what's in it. And if more than one drop falls into the bowl, I have to throw it away and start over." She was nodding importantly, and Nong was nodding along with her.

She begged Aunt Oom to tell her what was in the Secret Sauce. But Aunt Oom said, "Your stomach won't sing if the secret's not a secret. Didn't anybody ever tell you that before?"

Nong kept thinking of the Secret Sauce. And just before she went home that night, she sneaked behind the counter to get the red bottle.

But it was gone. Nong searched everywhere, and then suddenly Aunt Oom was right beside her, looking down.

"I knew you'd be back here," said Aunt Oom. "That's the way people are. They return to the scene of the secret. So I moved the bottle, way up to the highest shelf I could find. The shelf is so high, even I can't reach it. That's where the sauce is now—way up high, out of reach. Which, after all, is where a secret should be."

She smiled at Nong and went off to clean the big copper pot.

Cat on the Neck (And Other Remedies)

ONE DAY Nong got a piece of chili in her eye. She was in the back room at Aunt Oom's, chopping, when it happened.

Aunt Oom always had odd jobs for Nong. She had to mop the floor and wipe tables.

"Cleanliness," said Aunt Oom. "That's the key to success in the soup trade, Nong."

Nong refilled the containers of sugar and fish sauce for the customers to put in their soup. She washed the chopsticks and spoons. Nong enjoyed doing these things. They were parts of the soup trade, too.

She also liked chopping chilies. It was a new skill for her. Oi had shown her how to chop quickly, so that all of the pieces would be the same size. And she had warned Nong to always chop safely.

Aunt Oom had stood by, nodding. "Safety first," she had said. "That's another key to success."

Now Aunt Oom was out front, stirring the big copper pot full of broth. Oi was serving the soup. The men liked to smile at her as she put down their bowls on the tables.

In the back room, Nong was careful to keep her fingers clear of the knife while she chopped. She bent down low over the cutting board.

Oi came to the door of the room. "I've never seen you concentrate so hard," she said. "You look like I do when I'm ironing."

Nong looked up at her sister and smiled. When she looked back down and chopped again, that's when one of the pieces of chili flew up into her eye.

At first she was not sure what had happened. Her eye watered. Then it started to burn.

She wanted to cry out, but there were customers in the front room.

"Oi," she said as quietly as she could. "Help me." She rubbed her eye with her hands. But some of the juice from the chilies had gotten on her fingers, and that made her eye sting even more. "It hurts."

Oi tried to look in Nong's eye. "I'll go get Aunt Oom."

Aunt Oom came back wringing her hands on her apron. "Chili in the eye," she said. "Happens all the time to soupmakers' assistants." She was speaking calmly. "The first thing to do is to get you out of this room. It's best to get away from the scene of the accident."

Aunt Oom and Oi walked Nong to a table out front. The customers turned around toward her. Nong could not see them because her eyes were closed and full of tears.

"Chili in the eye," Aunt Oom told the customers. "No problem. Your soup's coming up in a minute."

The customers stayed turned around, watching. Suddenly their soup did not seem so important.

"Wash her eye out with rainwater," one of them said. "That's the best cure for chili."

"Make her sit with her face over a pot of steaming hot water," said an older man who sat near the big copper pot. "That will sweat the sting out."

"That's not the best way," said a man in the corner. "Hold her

upside-down, and count by nines to a hundred. That's what my mother always did."

Aunt Oom did none of these things. She went to the counter and returned with a spoonful of salt.

"Open up," she told Nong, who still had her eyes closed. "Open up, but don't swallow." Aunt Oom put the salt in Nong's mouth.

Nong made a face and almost coughed out the salt. But as she sat there, she felt the sting in her eye start to fade.

Meanwhile, the customers kept talking.

"What's the best way to loosen a fish bone that's stuck in your throat?" someone asked.

"Get a cat to rub the back of your neck," said the man in the corner confidently.

"No, no," said the man who had suggested the rainwater. "You cross your eyes and breathe in the scent of fresh lemon."

"You're both wrong," said the man near the big copper pot. "You sit with your face over steaming hot water. That will sweat the bone out."

Aunt Oom finished making their soup and came back over to Nong. "How's your eye now?"

"It's better," Nong tried to say, but her mouth was still full of salt. She went to the back room and washed it out several times.

Nong came back out to Aunt Oom. "It's much better," she said. "How did you know what to do?"

Aunt Oom was scooping some broth out of her big copper pot. "You're not the first person to get chili in your eye. Lots of people have suffered before you."

"But how could you know to use salt?"

Aunt Oom winked at Nong. "I've been around a long time. I've learned things." She dipped some noodles into steaming hot water. "Keep your eyes and your ears open. You'll learn things, too."

Nong stood at the counter and watched her. "What would you do if you got salt in your eye? Would you have to suck on a chili?"

"I don't think that would work. Salt has a cure of its own."

Before Nong could ask what it was, the customers saw her.

"Look. There's the eye girl. She's better now."

"The salt did the trick after all."

"Steaming hot water would have worked just as well."

Nong blinked at them. The customers still looked a little blurry.

"I don't get it," said the rainwater man. "What does her mouth have to do with her eye?"

"They're connected," said the man in the corner. "If you keep rice in your mouth while you slice onions, you won't cry."

"Ah, go on."

"It's true," said the man who liked steaming hot water. "The body is full of connections. Your eyes and your mouth. Your head and your hands. The teeth and the soles of your feet." He chewed for a moment. "And, of course, your nose and your stomach." The man bent down close to his soup and kept eating.

That night at home, Nong told her mother that she'd gotten chili in her eye. "I'm better now, though."

Her mother, who was slicing cabbage and cooking some soup of her own, looked at Nong's eye. "It looks fine," she said. "Aunt Oom had you chew on red onions, I take it. It's about time you learned how to cure common problems."

She put the cabbage in the boiling soup water, and the steam rose into their faces.

The Secret Sauce

WORKING AT THE SOUP SHOP was fine while it lasted. When summer vacation came, Nong and Oi helped out every day. Being around soup all the time made them cheerful and calm.

"It's good for the teeth, too," claimed Aunt Oom as she ladled out broth from the big copper pot.

Then one day Aunt Oom called them into the back room and told them she was closing the shop. "I've been at this for years, and I've made enough money. Enough's enough. Besides, look at my hands." She held them out. They were wrinkled and pink, the result of working so closely with broth.

It was strange to see Aunt Oom standing anywhere but beside the big pot. As she stood in the crowded back room, she seemed to cast more than her share of shadows.

"But your soup is special," said Oi.

"Nonsense! Soup is soup," said Aunt Oom, even though she had told them time after time that no one could make broth with a snap to it like she could.

"But what about you?" said Nong. "We'll miss you."

"Oh, nonsense again. I'm just an old soupmaker. What's more commonplace than that?" And she hurried off to dish out more soup.

On the last day, Aunt Oom told them her plan. "Everyone eats free today," she said. "Word will get around, and by this afternoon we'll be packed with people." She smiled at the idea. "It's my way to say thank you. I want to give something back."

Nong and Oi prepared even more sliced pork and vegetables than usual.

"We should have gotten her something," said Nong as they worked. "To make sure she'll remember us."

Oi nodded. "That would have been nice. But it's hard for a kid to give gifts to a soupmaker."

Before she could explain, the first customers came—two men. They were the same two men whose stomachs had danced and sung on Nong's first day on the job. The men ate their soup, which was full of extra pork, and then they pulled out their money.

Aunt Oom came out from beside the copper pot and went to their table.

"Today's my last day," she told them. "The soup's on me."

"Last day?" said the men. "How can it be? Where will we go to eat soup? What will become of our stomachs?"

"I've made up my mind," said Aunt Oom. "Please accept the soup as a gift. Would you like two more bowls?"

The men shook their heads. "We don't want free soup. We insist on paying. In fact, we want to pay double!" They put money down on the table and walked out before Aunt Oom could stop them. They took a long look at the big copper pot as they passed it, and then they went out to the street.

"Well, that didn't work out," said Aunt Oom.

Soon more customers came, and they insisted on paying double, too. "To thank you for years of your soup," they said. Before long word had spread, and the shop was full of people paying all kinds of money.

"Well," joked Aunt Oom, "if I had known this would happen, I would have quit long ago." But in the back room, where Oi was slicing more and more pork, Aunt Oom said, "That idea backfired. Look at all this money we're making!"

That night Nong and Oi finished cleaning and went to say good-night. It was later than usual. Aunt Oom was sitting at a table out front, counting money. "This is all going straight to the temple, first thing tomorrow," she said. "The best thing to do with a gift is keep giving it."

Nong stood and watched her. "Aunt Oom," she said, and she fidgeted. "Since this is your last day, why don't you tell me what's in the Secret Sauce?"

"The Secret Sauce? Why, I had forgotten that I told you about that." Aunt Oom stood up. "Close your eyes. You, too, Oi." Almost immediately, she said, "Now open them."

She was standing in front of them holding the red bottle.

"I never told anybody about this before," she said. "I'll tell you how secret this is. It's so secret that nobody else even knows a Secret Sauce exists."

"You mean it's just us?" asked Nong.

"That's right."

"Wow!" Nong looked at Oi, who was staring at the red bottle, too, even though she was a teenager.

"Can you guess what's in it?" said Aunt Oom.

"It must be a drug," said Oi, who had been taught about drugs in high school.

"Some kind of perfume," said Nong.

Aunt Oom laughed. "You're going to be disappointed. Here. I'll give you a taste."

She brought out a spoon and poured out some of the Secret Sauce.

Oi tasted it; so did Nong.

"Do you know?"

"Another taste," said Nong. Aunt Oom poured out a new spoonful.

Nong tasted it slowly. Her taste buds were trying to remember.

"It's coconut cola," she said at last.

"That's right," said Aunt Oom. "See? You're disappointed now, aren't you?"

"How can one drop of coconut cola change the flavor of a whole bowl of soup?"

"Who knows? How can one smile change your whole day? But listen. On the first day I opened this shop, a drop of coconut cola accidentally fell into the first bowl of soup that I made. Just by chance. That bowl was for Mr. Pu, by the way. He was my very first customer. He ate that bowl up and ordered another. Ever since then, I've put a drop in every bowl that I made."

"It's like a superstition."

"Yes," said Aunt Oom. "But it was a secret. That's what made it so powerful." She paid them from the money on the table, and she gave them a bonus, besides.

"What are you going to do now?" said Oi. "You'll have so much free time." Her hands were gripping the pay tightly.

"I'm going to travel the world! I'll take my copper pot and eat soup in every town that I come to! The Soup Queen, that's me!" Aunt Oom smiled. "Or maybe I'll sit in my back room talking to neighbors. It's cool there, you know."

Nong was still thinking about the Secret Sauce as she walked home beside Oi. "I can't believe it was coconut cola."

"I can," said Oi. "I could taste it right from the first bowl I ever ate there."

"No, you couldn't. It was only one drop."

"I could."

"Couldn't!"

Oi raised her eyebrows innocently at her younger sister. "Well, there's no way to prove it now, is there?" Holding tightly to their money, she ran on ahead down the lane.

Songkran

Nong was like any other kid on Songkran Day. Songkran is the name of Thailand's old New Year's Day, which has a special tradition. On that day, people can throw water at one another, and no one minds. In fact, they expect it, and they laugh when it happens.

Songkran comes on April 13, which in Thailand is in the middle of the summer. The water is welcome as a way to cool off.

Nong went down to the end of the lane, beside Aunt Ray's stand. Her friends were already there, filling big buckets with water. Each friend used a plastic bowl as a scoop. They filled the buckets and sat by the side of the road, waiting.

Whenever anyone passed, they were ready. They filled their scoops with water and poured it over the people who came by on bicycles and motorcycles. "Happy Songkran," they yelled out. The bicyclists went on, then got drenched again by the next group of kids down the street.

Songkran made good sense to Nong. The idea was to wash away the sins and the bad luck of the old year, and make everyone clean for the new one. It was a way to start over, refreshed. Nong liked that idea. Wash out what's old; let new things take root.

When no one passed by, Nong and her friends poured water on

one another. Puddles formed all around them. Someone had brought powder, too. They used it to scent the water. They rubbed it on one another's faces.

Nong was the busiest pourer. She could duck down and sneak up on people, and when motorcyclists passed, she had good aim. She poured so much water that she ran out of breath and had to sit down. It reminded her of the workmen who took breaks from digging trenches. Then she was back up and pouring again.

There were only a few rules for Songkran. You could not pour water over the heads of older people, just over their hands, and even then, gently. You could not throw water at people who were riding with small children, either. That was too dangerous.

Everyone else was fair game. In the market on Songkran, people walked around with wet shirts and hair. They had blotches of powder on their cheeks. None of the sellers minded, of course. It was their custom, too.

Usually, Nong's group stayed off to the side of the road. Only the Different Boy went out in the middle. He took off his shirt and waved it at motorcycles, like a matador waving a flag at a bull. He waited until one motorcycle passed, then ran down the road after it. He got some ice cubes and poured the cold water down the shirts of the drivers.

"You're making it dangerous," said a girl who lived along that part of the road. "You're not supposed to be mean."

The Different Boy laughed. "It's Songkran. I'm just having fun."

Nong saw the accident happen. She was taking a rest on a bench under a tree when one of their teachers rode up. They greeted him and poured water over his hands politely.

"Hey, that's no fun," said the teacher, who was wearing a T-shirt and sweatpants. "Pour it on me for real. I want to get wet. That's why I wore these old clothes."

One by one, Nong's friends grew braver. They poured water over the teacher's shoulders and down the back of his neck. Nong joined in, too.

"That's more like it," said the teacher. "That's what Songkran is all about." He waved to them and began to ride away.

They were waving to him and saying, "Happy Songkran," when the motorcycle came up from behind. They were not expecting it. Only the Different Boy was ready.

Suddenly he jumped out from their group, right in the path of the motorcycle. "Ha!" he shouted, and he threw water into the rider's face.

The rider was a woman. When she swerved away from the Different Boy, her tires slid through the puddles. The woman screamed as the water hit her face. The motorcycle fell over and slid down the road toward the teacher.

They ran after her. The teacher got off his bicycle and went over. All of them were dripping onto the roadway.

The woman was holding her arm. She had scraped it badly when she hit the ground. Spots of blood were mixing in with the water on the road.

"Are you all right?" asked the teacher. "What happened?"

They picked up her motorcycle and wheeled it to the side of the road. There were a lot of scratch marks.

The woman was standing up slowly.

"I guess I'm OK," she said. She was rubbing her arm and wincing.

"How did that happen?" said the teacher. He turned to them. "I thought you were playing politely."

Nong and her friends looked at the Different Boy.

"We were," he said. "We were playing politely."

One of the girls pointed to the woman's arm. "That isn't playing politely."

"It isn't my fault," said the Different Boy. "We were all playing together."

"Well," said the teacher. "Since you were all playing together, I think all of you should apologize to this woman. And if she needs any help, you're all responsible." He looked at the woman's arm again and shook his head. "I'm disappointed in you," he told them. "This isn't the idea of Songkran."

"We're sorry," they said to the woman.

"We didn't mean it," the Different Boy added.

The teacher talked with the woman for a few minutes. They both rode off slowly. The teacher looked over his shoulder at them as he rode away down the street.

Nong and her friends went back to the buckets. The Different Boy came over to join them.

"No," said the girl who lived there. "You don't know how to play Songkran."

"I didn't do anything," said the Different Boy. "It wasn't my fault."

"It isn't fun when you play. Go away."

The Different Boy stood watching as they scooped out more water. "I was just playing," he told them. "This is Songkran."

He watched them for a while. Then he took a bucket and went on down the street. He stood by himself at the side of the road.

Nong and her friends sat and watched as a motorcycle came toward them. The rider slowed down, waiting to get splashed. They let him go by. He gave an odd smile and went on down the road.

"What's the matter?" they said. "Why didn't we get him?"

Down the street, they heard a big "Ha!" The Different Boy's water splashed against the motorcycle, and he laughed. He looked up toward Nong's group and laughed again, louder.

Nong and her friends went on sitting there.

"Hey," said somebody finally. "Come on. It's Songkran."

Time to let new things take root.

Check

NONG'S MOTHER had had many jobs. She used to sell cold drinks at the primary school down the street. She sold coconut juice, salted lemonade, and juices made from berries and pineapples and limes. Every morning she pushed her cart full of juices to the school, and the children rushed out to buy them at lunchtime. Then she waited in the shade until school was dismissed, and the children rushed out again.

But that school was converted into government offices. The government officials never rushed to do anything. The profits from selling the drinks dwindled.

After that she sold fried bananas. She worked grilling chicken livers, too. For a while she helped out at a fruitstand.

Now she had a job selling custard.

Every day she prepared a dessert made from custard and sweet sticky rice. She went to sell it at the market. She wrapped each serving in a banana leaf, then slipped a splinter of wood, like a toothpick, through the leaf to keep it closed. Each packet contained three or four mouthfuls.

Nong's job was to tear pieces of banana leaf into sections, so that they would be ready for her mother to wrap around the custard. Sometimes Nong went along to the market. Soon she had learned how to wrap the sections of banana leaf herself.

"Fold it neatly," her mother had taught her the first day. "Like this."

Nong learned to fold the leaf with no bulges.

"Fold it quickly," her mother said then. "Like this."

Step by step, Nong was learning how to sell custard.

Her mother waited calmly until a customer came. Then her hands became busy. She could scoop out the rice, pour on some sweet coconut milk, and add a spoonful of custard much faster than Nong could fold the banana-leaf sections.

Her mother said it was important to show customers that each packet of custard was made fresh. "If they're satisfied, they'll come back tomorrow."

They got a few coins for each packet. When they had sold all the custard, they carried the pots home and got ready to make a batch to sell the next day.

"There's more to selling custard than meets the eye," said her mother.

One day after they had gone home, Nong sat tearing off sections of banana leaf—she could do that quickly and neatly now, too—when a man came to their house. He was from the school where Nong's father had worked. He handed a check to Nong's mother.

"This is from your husband's insurance fund," he said.

"It's over a year since he died," said Nong's mother.

"It took us a while to get through the paperwork."

Nong's mother looked at the check. "It's not much, is it."

"No, it isn't," said the man. "But it's something."

Nong's father had worked as a handyman at a school closer to town. The school was made of wood, so it always needed repairs. He could fix leaks and replace old planks cheerfully. He rode to work on a bicycle early every morning to make sure the building was ready for studying. He was on good terms with the dogs at the school, too, so he could prevent them from growling at students.

Nong and her mother studied the check after the man went away. Oi came and looked, too.

"Well, what should we get?" asked Nong.

"Let's think about that after dinner," said their mother. She sent Nong to the main road to buy pineapple curry.

Out in the lane Nong met the Buffalo Woman, making her way home with Coconut.

Nong walked along with them. "Suppose somebody gave you some money," she said.

"Why would they want to do that?"

"Just suppose. What would you buy?"

The Buffalo Woman shook her head. "I wouldn't know what to buy. I don't know what there is."

"If you had to. "

"If I had to? I don't know. Another buffalo, I guess. Why?"

Nong walked along with the Buffalo Woman a while longer. But soon she found herself heading to see Mr. Pu. She went up to the wide-open door and looked in.

Mr. Pu was sitting on the floor, eating jello.

"Suppose somebody gave you some money," said Nong.

Mr. Pu's spoon stopped in midair. "Say that again."

"Suppose somebody gave you some money."

Mr. Pu started nodding. "Money," he said. "Funny you should ask about that. Funny you should ask while I'm eating jello."

He put his spoon down and settled in to explain.

"You see, I was born back in the days before money. Shows you how old I am, doesn't it? I can still remember when money was invented. It was just about this time of day. Suddenly we had all this money. And nobody knew what to do with it! At first we just looked it over. Then we gave it away. Everybody did that. We used to give so much money away, and we got so much of it back, that all of us were millionaires at once. That's how money got started."

Nong had learned to wait until Mr. Pu paused in his stories for breath. Then she asked a new question.

"Did you buy anything?"

Mr. Pu pointed to the bowl on the floor. "Why, I used to buy jello. I bought all the jello I could find. I watched it wiggle a while, and then I gave that away, too." He smiled at her and went back to eating. As Nong turned to leave, she could see jello wiggling on Mr. Pu's spoon.

By the time Nong got home with the pineapple curry, Oi and her mother were waiting.

"The curry stand isn't that far away," said her mother.

Oi gave her a look, too. "Our rice is almost dried out."

Nong gave them the pineapple curry and said nothing. Worrying about drying-out rice was a sign that Oi was nearly grown up.

Nong's mother kept the check opened up by her plate while they ate.

"It isn't much money," she said finally. "But I guess we'll be able to get something." She ate some pineapple curry. "It would be nice to have a cement floor."

"Do we have enough?" said Oi. "Could we get tiles, too?"

"I don't know. I don't know how much things like that cost."

It was true. All of them knew the price of the things that they bought at the market—chili peppers and garlic, a sack of rice—but they could not even guess how much it cost to make a cement floor.

"What about a TV?" said Nong.

"Well, if we don't have a cement floor, where would we sit when we watched it?"

"But if we don't have a TV, what would we do when we sat on the cement floor?"

"Maybe we could get both."

"Is there enough?"

"Maybe. I don't know. Maybe not."

They went back to the curry and the almost-dried rice.

Then their mother stopped eating and sighed. "You know what I wish. When I was young my mother used to take me to market downtown. I loved to go to the silk shops. We never bought any, but I just liked being around it. I've always dreamed of selling silk."

"Why don't we do that, then?" said Oi. "We could help you."

"No," said their mother. "There's not nearly enough."

"We could borrow the rest," said Oi. "I could be a model."

"I could help, too," said Nong. "I could fold the pieces of silk."

"A silk shop!"

They were excited for a moment. Selling silk was something they had never considered before.

But their mother was shaking her head. "We could never do that. It's too big a risk. We should use it for something safer. Maybe for your education."

Now they were not so excited.

"I like the idea of a silk shop," said Oi.

Nong was watching Oi and her mother. "Why don't you ask me what I'd get?"

"What's that?"

Nong felt herself beginning to smile. "I'd buy some buffaloes."

"Buffaloes?" said Oi. "What for?"

"To take care of," said Nong. "Or how about a houseful of jello?" She couldn't help laughing. She was picturing it all wiggling.

But Oi was shaking her grown-up head. "You're not helping. You're just being silly."

"Well, we should do something soon," said Nong. "There's a drop of curry on the check already."

Her mother wiped off the curry with a tissue. "Enough about this. Let's eat."

She folded the check—neatly and quickly—and held it tightly while they finished the pineapple curry.